MW01609982

12 Tales of Christmas Horrors

Essel Pratt

Essel/

Embrace the Chaos!

Cover Art by

Copyright.

Essel Pratt

©2020, **Essel Pratt**

Table of Contents

Acknowledgement

To Christmas Lore and the mind of a horror writer.
.

The Deal That Saved Christmas

A savage rain bit at the flesh as December's frigid breeze slapped the face of a those too busy with holiday chores to notice the cloudburst. On this Christmas Eve the hustle and bustle was in full swing and emotions had changed from joyous cheer to anxious despair. The droves of last minute shoppers crowded the shops while tempers surpassed common sense. The snowless, yet soggy, winter did nothing to help raise spirits of holiday elation.

Outside upon the sidewalks, carolers could be heard on the street corners singing out of tune songs of goodwill towards man and faux hallelujahs. As cars drove by, water that had collected around the clogged drains splashed the less than jubilant chorales. On the opposite corner, Atheist protestors chanted against the commercialism of the season and the false prophet that the factions replaced with an obese elf during the month that their savior was supposedly born, in an attempt to demonstrate the ridiculousness of religion.

Amongst all of the noise and constant movement, a lone man sat quietly on a bench directly across the street of "Ye Ole Toy Store". His clothing gave the impression as though it was once an elaborate Santa suit. Miserably, the filthy coat and pants revealed the tattered seams and matted fur lining instead of the opulence it once displayed. As he sat there quietly on the hoary bench, he clutched his rain soaked and floppy hat in one hand while stroking his silvery white matted beard with the other. His presence was seemingly ignored by all passersby.

The old man's thoughts drifted to better times; times when the holiday focus was on the well being of family and friends and not who wins the battle for the last doll that defecates violently in a diaper. Tears blended with the rain that fell down his face from his exposed balding head. So lost in thought he was, he had not even noticed the little girl that sat quietly beside him.

The rain seemed to repel from the girl's jet black hair and her coatless body was unfazed by the chill in the blustery air. She sat quietly and stared into the old man's eyes. Within the black of his pupil, she could almost see his past and the joy he once experienced around the once joyous time of year. The faded blinding twinkle of his eyes could be seen buried in the back, waiting for a spark to ignite it once again. As the tears gently flowed through his wrinkles, they splashed to his lap only to mix with the cold rain.

The young girl reached out and gently placed her small hand on top of his. A magical sensation created a spark within her. The electricity was calming and revitalizing. However, to the man it was a shock to his system. His body jerked with confusion. Who was it that woke him from his thoughts? He had sat here, unnoticed, for days with only his thoughts to keep him company and the facade of existence to keep him sane.

As he glanced down at the strange little girl, she responded with an innocent smile. He had been invisible to the world for years, and as lonely as it was he had begun to accept it. He managed to crack a simple smile back at the child.

"Mr., why are you so sad?" asked the child in a quizzical tone. Her voice was soft and calming.

"Me? Uh, I'm just sitting here minding my own business", said the old man in a forced jolly tone, although you could hear the sadness in his voice. "Why have you chosen to sit here and bother me? I have come here for years to sit and collect my thoughts, and nobody has even glanced in my direction"

The child ignored his hollow words and responded with another query, "What is your name?"

"I should be asking you the same. Do you know how rude it is for a child to ask such questions of a man that is just trying to mind his own business? Where are your parents? And where is your coat? This rain will be the death of you!"

The child did not respond. She just stared at him blankly. Her eyes seemed to make him uncomfortable. "Why are you just staring at me? Now go away. I want to be left alone."

"Nick? That is your name, isn't it? Why do you always come here? These people just make you sad, don't they?" Rhetoric cursed the question as she stared, not expecting an answer in return.

"Wha! But how...how did you know my name? Nobody has called me that in what seems like almost an eternity, my dear. Hell, I have been practically nonexistent for a very long time. Who are you, and why are you bothering me?" Nick's tone seemed to express a hint of fear.

The rain on his forehead began to intermix with a cold sweat. His tears had dried up but the redness still occupied the white of his eyes. The little girl was right, though. Spending uninterupted hours within the this small town every year just made him sad. Sometimes he felt as though he should end it all, if only he could. Maybe that is why he chose the town. Maybe he hoped that someone would notice him and end his sadness for him.

"Paige…I am Paige", said the little girl, sounding like she was lost in thought. "I don't mean to pester you. I have just always wanted to meet you. I have watched you for so long. Your sadness confuses me. And the feeling I got when I touched your hand was unlike anything I have ever experienced. There was…happiness."

"What do you mean you have always wanted to meet me? And how did you know my name?" Nick was beginning to get frustrated with the Paige's rhetorical musings. "I just want to be left alone!"

"Alone? But, your very existence is due to your love of others. How can you just turn your back and walk away"? Her questions needed no answers. In fact, he had asked himself these questions on a daily basis.

Nick's sadness had plagued him for many years. It had become such a routine that he had almost forgotten what it was like to be happy. In fact, the only happy thought was that he could still feel at all.

"Why did you do it"? Paige seemed to know things about him that no other living being knew. He was actually becoming uncomfortable.

Nick did not answer. As he sat there, the frigid rain soaked suit weighed on him. It was so heavy he could barely move or he would have just walked away. He stared back at the child. Her skin, although bare, showed no sign of being cold at all. She moved very little, unless to look in his direction, or back at the ground. Her arms were folded neatly in her lap. As he observed her, his eyes met hers. In an instant, he noticed that her eyes were jet black with a thin iridescent blue outlining where her pupil should be. It was the iridescence that pierced his soul, he could feel it. He felt that he should be frightened but he wasn't. For the first time in a long time he felt calm and relieved.

"Who are you, really?" he asked. He almost felt at peace asking the question.

Paige did not answer. Instead she looked away towards the toy shop across the street. Kids rushed in and out of the shop with electronic whizzing and whirling toys in hand. Each child bragged of their finds trying to show off to one another. The parents boasted of how much they spent on each child and how they got the last popular toy on the shelf.

To the left of the doorway a small boy was sobbing uncontrollably. The rain seemed to amplify his sniffling. Nick heard the sniveling and glanced in his direction. A couple of older boys were there with him and poking fun. They could be heard calling him a baby because he believed in Santa Claus. They told him that Santa was not real, and even if he was real Santa would not visit him in the foster home. As the boy cried harder, the rain seemed to increase in intensity and drowned out his whining.

Nick looked back at Paige, as the tears started to run down his face again. He felt the boy's sadness. He wanted to help, but couldn't. Paige stared back at him and asked, "Nick, why did you sell your soul?"

Nick understood why Paige was here. He knew that she did not have a name but was in fact a Paige from the depths of Hell. "For the kids, I did it for the kids." Nick's voice vibrated as his lip quivered.

He was ashamed of what he had become. His past used to be full of such happiness as he brought joy to the lives of others. His personality was contagious. When he was around, people would gather to listen to his stories and laugh at his jokes. Travelers from all over would share his stories when they arrived home. He had become a celebrity of his time. He never asked for the notoriety, but it did help with his cause. His goal was to spread joy and goodwill to all that were around. He found that children were fond of his wood carvings, so he began to give them away.

He found that he was giving them away faster than he could make them, so he decided to hold off until he had plenty to give away at once. Nick hid away in his small cabin deep in the woods. The peacefulness let him focus on the task at hand. He spent all spring, summer, and autumn carving his creations. On the first sunny day of December, he traveled to town to pass out his gifts. Although it was sunny, it was still cold, so he put on his best red fur coat and pants with matching hat and gloves. He hooked his horses to his sleigh and rode into town. It was such a hit that he turned it into a tradition. If a child wasn't home, he would hide the present under their blankets for them to find when they returned.

Eventually, the hidden presents became the preferred method. The parents got so much joy by the surprised looks on the children's faces, that they invited Nick to stop by at night. They would leave their doors open so he could sneak in and leave the presents near the fireplaces. The smaller presents would be wrapped in the socks that were hung to dry.

Nick's thoughts of the old days brought brightness back to his cheeks. The sparkle that once twinkled in his eye was returning and his stoic expression actually cracked a real smile. He looked back at the Paige, and his smile faded once again. He felt the sadness take control once again.

The Paige stared back, seemingly searching for the glimmer that she witnessed for a brief moment. She was in awe of Nick. He was everything she wished she could be, but knew it was impossible. The darkness within her was too black for a light to shine through. A demon of her nature had never experienced existence, therefore has never had the privilege of feeling emotion, pain, or being. However, she could feel curiosity, and that curiosity is what brought her here.

"Nick, you seemed so happy. Why did you do it?" Nick knew what the Paige was speaking of. His thoughts, once again, traveled to the past, to a time that he had hoped never to visit again.

***

Nick looked forward to visiting the town and hiding presents every year. He had become known as Mr. Claus amongst the children. He made sure that he always wore the same red suit and even adorned his sleigh with bells so the children could hear him coming at night. His visits had become the highlight of the year. The Parents would even plan a feast around his arrival and decorate the houses in anticipation.

However, as his body aged it became harder for him create new toys every year, let alone make the journey. On what he feared would be his final year, he took special care to add additional detail to his creations. Some even had moving parts. His tired hands had become shaky, yet he managed to finish the toys ahead of time.

Nick managed to load his sleigh with the gifts, but his body was too weak to pull himself into the seat. As he strained to hoist himself, he collapsed onto the soft snowy ground below. When he awoke he was inside near the fire. The fire was warmer than it had ever been and the glow was more intense. He surveyed his surroundings and noticed a strange man was sitting across from him. Before he had a chance to speak, the man motioned to a hot cup of tea in front of him.

"Drink the tea, Nick. It will help you regain your strength."   Nick was still shook up and confused. "Go on, it should be cooled down enough to drink. Oh my, where are my manners", said the tall, slender man.

His facial features seemed cloaked by the intense light of the fire. "I found you outside lying in the snow. I had thought you were dead for sure. I brought you in and thought I would stay by your side until you awoke. I hope that was ok," the voice was calm yet as distant as though the man was not here at all. Nick thought it was because he was not completely coherent just yet.

The man admired the toy collection, "You really do love the children, don't you? What would you say if I could help you deliver these fine gifts to not just the children in town, but also in cities across the world? You would like that, wouldn't you?" This was not a question that was meant to be answered, the man knew of Nick's dreams.

"Nick...before you sip on your tea, let me ask you something. If I could grant you immortality, a lifetime of giving gifts to children, would you accept? As a bonus, what if I could give you access to magical steeds that can fly you around the world on your sleigh? That could expand your reach? Would you accept?" The man's voice hinted at a mysterious excitement.

Nick could not speak, he could only stare and dream. The man continued, "what if I could grant visibility to the mystic creatures all around us, some of which are willing to help you create new toys and dolls? Would you accept?"

An infatuation with the idea of helping thousands, no millions, of kids filled his mind. He could almost feel youth sweep through his frail body. "All you have to do is drink the tea to accept my offer. All I ask in return is your soul. Don't worry though; what does an immortal man need a soul for? Hell, God will probably grant you Sainthood for helping so many children, anyway."

Sainthood, immortality, and an eternity of bringing joy to children, what more was there to think about? Nick's shaky hands picked up the hot tea. As he brought it closer to his lips, the fire intensified. He sipped on the tea and felt energy erupt inside of him. He couldn't stop drinking; in fact he threw back the cup of tea as though it was a shot of whiskey. As the last drop hit his tongue, the fire subsided to its usual glow and the mystery man was gone.

With newfound energy, Nick quickly rushed to his sleigh. His horses had been replaced with a majestic breed of reindeer. He jumped in and seemed to fly to the town in no time flat. In just seconds, all the toys had been delivered and he was on his way home.

As he arrived home, a crowd of peculiar creatures stood outside his door. They looked like humans, only miniature. He welcomed them to his home and soon found they were a race of mystic woodland creatures that specialized in woodworking. They had admired his handiwork

for years and were excited at the chance to help
him.

***

Once again, the light within him spread
throughout. The Paige marveled at the glow. Her
stare brought Nick back to reality and once again
the light faded. "You have immortality and yet you
choose to spend it wallowing in self-pity. Why
would you do such a thing?" The Paige was
inquisitive as to why someone with everything they
could ever imagine would choose this path.

"It was all taken from me, everything. For
years I and my elven helpers, would create
wonderful toys and deliver them to the world.
Each year, just before my journey, the faceless man
that granted me my gift would visit. He would

praise me for my work and thank me for my pure soul. Then he would leave without even a whiff of his existence. Then, as electronic toys gained popularity over my simple wooden creations, the elves and I made fewer and fewer toys. The love for us seemed to fade", said Nick as he remembered how his world was thrown into a turmoil. "Finally, we found that parents had begun to compete between each other. They would brag about who bought better toys. I was becoming disgusted with the way the holiday turned to greed. I guess my soul could sense my anger. As it festered in the depths of the faceless man's Hell, it began to take the shape of evil. Its pureness was easily overcome by the screams of Hell. That year, the man did not visit. Instead my soul came back, it hungered for vengeance. It was jealous that I had chosen this life of everlasting happiness over my own being. The demon that I created ravaged my workshop. The elves were all tortured and extinguished. Their dismembered bodies were strewn all across the shop. None survived the rampage… what had I created?"

Nick's emotions overflowed with grief. He replayed the scenario in his head every year. He searched for an answer, a way to fix things. However, the greediness around him showed him that the old ways could never return.

"Nick, what if I told you that I could help you? What if I could bring back your light, no strings attached?"

"Why should I trust you? You are a demon, are you not?"

"I may be a creature from the depths of Hell, but I bare no ill will. I have seen your light and your darkness fight for control within your depths. I have never seen such a battle in all of my eternities. Your light intrigues me." The Paige seemed to show a hint of emotion as she talked. "When I touched your hand earlier, I felt something that I have never felt before. There was an energy that flowed through me, I felt alive for a split second. I actually felt the joy in your heart. I know that I will never feel that again, but you have given me a gift, please let me help you."

"I would do anything to gain my old life back, but I have nothing left to give. I'm sorry, I just cannot be helped." A feeling of worthlessness spread over him.

"Here, take this wooden plane. It was the last toy your top elf made before his life was taken." The plane was a simple design painted in red with black accents. "Give it to the young boy across the way; he is fascinated by planes of all types. After you present your gift, touch your nose and you will be whisked away home as though the tragedy that occurred had never happened. It is a gift from me to you."

Nick's hand trembled as he reached for the plane. What did he have to lose? As he clutched the plane in both hands, he stood from the bench and turned his back to the Paige. After a couple steps, he turned around slowly. The girl was still there. "Why did you come here today, after all of these years?", he asked in a hushed tone.

"Honestly, I came here to drag you to the depths of Hell for an eternity of torture and torment. You see, after I destroyed everything you loved, I thought I would be content to watch you suffer here on earth. I became a paige, bent on dragging those that disobeyed the terms of their contract, to Hell. The longer I watched you, the more I hungered to bring you down with me. I figured I would trick you into coming with me, but when I touched your hand I realized I was wrong. For the first time, I felt why you had to choose immortality over me…I felt happiness." With that final word, the Paige disappeared into nothingness.

Nick turned towards the boy. Each step that he took renewed his once opulent garb to its former glory. As he reached the young boy, his face lit up. "Santa Claus, is it really you?"

"It is my boy. I am sorry I have neglected your wishes for so long. Please accept this wooden plane. I am sorry it doesn't have flashing lights or motorized propellers," said Nick in a regretful tone.

"No, it is perfect! Thank you Santa!" The young boy hugged Nick to show his appreciation.

The warmth was returning to the old man's body. He had noticed that the rain had stopped and a steady snowfall began to cover the ground. The caroler's on the corner began to sing in tune and their manner was more cheerful. Even the loud Atheists had abandoned their post on the corner.

As he took one last look around the small town, he knew that things were changing for the better. The feeling of sorrow was fading fast. True to his old ways he yelled out, "Merry Christmas to all!" As he finished his greeting, his finger touched the tip of his nose. The world around him faded to black as he was whisked away to his old workshop, where he knew his elves would be to greet him.

The Soldier Carver Elf

Within the ranks of Santa's elves, there lived an elf named Deek. His emerald eyes and ruby hair stood out amongst the rest. Throughout the year he carved out wood and crafted soldiers that boys would unwrap on Christmas day, where they would reenact imaginary battles within their minds. Deek was the best of the soldier carvers and non could compare, but his heart was not in the work. Within his heart, his hopes, and his dreams, Deek dreamed of crafting ballerinas for girls and boys to open.

Deek pleaded his case with the head elf in charge, only to meet rejection each time. He cursed the order of elven assignments and sulked back to his worn in stool where blade met wood and a soldier was born, time and time again. As the years lingered on, the ornery blister upon his mind would integrate small imprints of his dream within the toys he'd create. At first it was a small gesture, nothing too abrupt, but instead a small ballerina outline within the removable caps, noticeable only by those that were looking for it. However, as his heart faded from devotion and the work became a job, imprints of his dreams became more outwardly, although still hidden from plain view.

The faces of the stoic soldiers were softer, their features more of beauty than war-torn despair. Their blistered fingers and drooping postures stood straight and defined with soft edges. The other elves praised him for improving his already rustic perfection to a more lifelike presentation, not realizing the battle hardened men under the uniforms had gradually transitioned to women tired of battle and ready to express their love of dance.

"Deek," called out the head elf in charge, beckoning him forth.

Deek trembled, worried his craftsmanship had revealed too much of his nonconformity as he scraped his feet across the floor with each step toward his boss. A cold sweat formed upon his brow and a lump gathered within his throat.

"Sir," Deek said in respect as he approached the head elf in charge.

"Deek," he began. "Santa is making a special visit to an orphanage tomorrow, where the boys inside have all been left behind as their fathers have perished in war. As a result of the painful losses, their mothers have all taken their lives and left the boys behind with no families to take care of them any longer. Therefore, Santa would like you, our best soldier carver, to create exact likenesses of their fathers that he may present to them. Here are pictures of their families for you to work from. I trust you can have this completed by tomorrow at noon's light?"

"Of course, sir," replied Deek. "It would be my honor."

Deek rushed back to his stool where ten blocks of the finest wood awaited his return. He laid out the pictures upon his bench, observing the happiness within the eyes of the children and their mothers but absorbing the sadness within the faces of the fathers. He realized the pictures were all taken just before the fathers left for war, knowing they would not be returning to their families again.

Sadness crept into Deek's heart and tears welled within his eyes. He sensed the grief the children felt as a result of losing both parents, not knowing how happiness might creep back into their lives again. As emotion overcame him, an idea crept into his mind.

Deek grabbed the first block of wood and scraped his metal blade against its façade, digging into the grain to make the body take shape. He chipped away as the lights of the workshop went dark and the murmuring of the other elves went silent as their shifts ended and he remained alone within the workspace. It was then that he jumped into overdrive, turning his idea into reality.

The wood bended to his will, becoming his greatest masterpieces of all time. It was the surprise inside that demanded his focus. Metalwork was not his expertise, although he had mingled with it for a few years as he broadened his skills to create the replica rifles the soldiers carried.

He worked through the night, until the morning shift turned the lights back on. When the head elf in charge arrived, he rushed over to Deek's bench and grasped the stoic soldiers within his grasp, turning them within his hands and comparing them to the pictures that scattered around the table.

"These are exquisite," he praised, while patting Deek upon the back. "They look exactly like the children's fathers. Well done, Santa will be forever grateful."

Deek grinned and raised his hand.

"Now, Deek, there is no need to raise your hand if you have a question. We're not in school any longer. What is it?" the head elf in charge continued to admire the soldiers.

"Well," he stumbled on his words. "I was wondering if I might accompany Santa on this trip and watch the children open the gifts. I would love nothing more than to see their faces, and of those around them, when the presents are unwrapped."

"That is a fantastic idea," replied the head elf in charge. "I shall ask Santa myself. I don't know his response, but I'd suggest you ready yourself, in case the answer is yes."

Deek rushed off to his room and changed from the dust-laden work clothes to his celebratory outfit that he wore only during special occasions. He hadn't more than slipped on his final show when a knock pounded upon his door. Anxious to hear the answer from the head elf in charge, he pulled the door open and dropped his jaw as Santa himself stood before him.

"I hear you would like to accompany me on my journey to deliver the toy soldiers," his voice was forever jolly.

"Yes, sir," Deek stuttered.

"I am leaving in ten minutes," replied Santa. "Be at the sleigh in five. I've looked over the soldiers and must say, they are your best work yet. You've definitely imprinted some joyous elf magic within. I would be honored if you were able to experience the smiles on the faces of the children as you make a difference within their lives."

Santa walked away, disappearing down the hall as Deek stood there in awe of the personal visit from Santa himself. As the shock wore off, he rushed from his room, slamming the door behind him, and hastening toward the sleigh. He arrived mere seconds before Santa.

"Please, dear Deek," said Santa as he took his seat behind the reigns. "Come aboard, we must be on our way."

***

Although their journey took them thousands of miles, it was only a mere seconds before the reindeer landed the sleigh at the front of a lonely brick building in a sad American city. He stared in disbelief as the thought of orphans living within was ever a good idea, rather than residing in the country where they could learn new skills and live life to its fullest, despite the despair within their hearts. They were being suffocated by oversight, just as he had as his dreams of crafting ballerinas were diminished by Santa and his management staff.

"Come now," urged Santa as he thrust the sack upon his back and ventured forth into the grime covered steel doors.

Deek followed, assaulted by the stench of filth within the building, sensing the sadness creep within his very soul.

"Do not become overwhelmed," said Santa, trying to calm him. "A spot of happiness is all that is needed to clear the cobwebs and ignite some cheer."

Deek was not convinced as he realized there was not a happy face to be found among the frowns and tears. He followed Santa into the gathering room, where a browning pine was covered in paper drawings and a popcorn chain. None were places with care, but seemed to have been thrown into place. A caregiver opened the blinds to allow the day's magnificence inside, only to make the room appear drearier as the dirty walls and stained tiles failed to reflect the light in any resemblance of beauty.

Santa bellowed out cheer from deep within his gut, praising the boys for their bravery and sacrifice. Non returned the cheer, seeming disinterested at their best. Sensing their hearts were not warming, Santa removed the presents from his bag and handed each to their corresponding boy.

"Go ahead," urged Santa. "Each has been personalized for you by my greatest elven craftsman here, Deek."

Deek watched on as the boys opened their gifts, sensing the sadness infiltrate their auras as the faces of their fathers looked back at them.

They turned the figures within their hands as silent wishes of reunion crept into their hearts.

"There is more," Deek blurted out.

"More?" Santa was curious.

"Yes," replied Deek. "There is a crease along the sides of each figure. Pull upon them to reveal another toy inside."

"Like a Russian doll?" queries Santa. "Brilliant. Go ahead boys, let's see what is inside."

The boys did as requested, pulling their fathers' likenesses in half to reveal the beauty of their mothers within. Tears welling up in their faces as they fought back the sobs of despair that welled within.

"Brilliant," replied Santa. "You've given them both their fathers and their mothers. A more perfect gift has never been created."

"My apologies for not telling you earlier," said Deek. "I was afraid you would disapprove, like you did with my desire to craft ballerinas."

"Don't be silly," replied Santa. "This is a special occasion, where something of this beauty would be welcomed. Not like your silly pipedream of creating toys for girls. Only the female elves are skilled enough for that. You are a boy and such silliness would never be thought of."

"Don't you think the depictions of the mothers are beautiful?" asked Deek.

"Of course," replied Santa. "But, you did have imaged to work from, so it is excused. Although, of you ever sneak something like this into a present again, you will be appropriately punished."

"Understood," said Deek. "I guess this would not be the best time to tell you there is another surprise inside the mother figures."

"Is there?" asked Santa. "Go ahead boys, open them up."

Deek took a step back from Santa and watched as the overwhelming air of depression failed to transition to happiness, yet the slightest glimmer of hope pressed the boys to delve deeper into the figures.

Santa stared in amazement as the boys revealed replica pistols that their fathers carried during war stuffed inside. "Pure genius! Another memento of the heroism of their fathers."

"Is it though?" asked Deek. "Or is it a reminder that the sadness within is crushing and that there is really only one way to escape it?"

"My dear Deek, I am not sure what you mean," said Santa as ten shots exploded on unison and the limp bodies of each boy fell to the floor. "What have you done? You hid real guns in the toys? How could you be so irresponsible?"

"Irresponsible?" asked Deek. "I don't see it that way. For years, I've asked to do one simple thing. I've asked to create beautiful ballerinas for boys and girls. In return, you've stolen that happiness and made me suffer while creating toys of war. You've stolen my happiness from me."

"Ballerinas are girl toys," replied Santa. "We've gone over this a thousand times."

"Today, you gave these boys the one thing they wanted the least in life; remembrance of their dead parents," replied Deek, not pausing after Santa spoke. There was no happiness left in their hearts, but you managed to offer them a path further into despair. So, I gave them a way out. If there was hope, a simple flag would have popped from the barrel and gave them a laugh. But if there was nothing left, the bullet was the final act. I used my elven magic to give them what they needed in life, even if that was death."

"That was not your choice," Santa yelled, jubilance absent from his voice.

"It was my choice," Deek replied, pulling another pistol from his pocket.

"Now, don't do anything foolish," demanded Santa.

"Too late, my happiness shall never return," said Deek, pulling the trigger as the barrel pressed against his own temple.

As the eleven bodies spread across the floor, puddles of blood outlining their forms, Santa stared in disbelief as caregivers rushed in and sirens sounded from outside. He drifted in the thought that the damnation before him was caused by a decision he made without consideration of Deek's own feelings. As tears ran down his cheeks, he meandered past the emergency crews and sobbing staff, lifting himself into the sleigh before pulling the reigns and heading home. The sadness that festered within, damned his ways of old and determined him to make a change within the workshops. No longer would toys of war be created. No longer would segregation of male and female norms be forced upon the children. It took a single elf's act of sacrifice to make him realize that happiness was not a binary concept, but instead fluid in the mind of the child.

Christmas Goose

Ebenezer Scrooge looked downward on the Christmas season, rejecting joyous gatherings, dismissing acts of good will toward men, and refusing to partake in compassionate regards for the human species, even for one month in the entire year. Costs of heating his office, the extra logs it took to keep the deathly sickness from intruding into his lungs, meant more work to make up for the money lost. In his youth, he battered through the winters with extra layers of clothing, refusing to give in to Old Man Winter's constant attack until spring gave way to warmth. Since three seasons prior, that was his tradition. Then, his lungs and chest became infected with influenza, forcing him bedridden for nearly the entire season as he battled the sickness. Since then, he decided his aged bones were just no match for the winter's hold and decided to stoke the fireplace as he worked harder to recover the lost profits.

During his bout with the sickness, Ebenezer Scrooge refused to shut down his business. He made his affluent living by lending money to those in need, with the expectation of a hefty attachment of interest in return. Oftentimes, those that borrowed repaid twofold. Even the bank, as full of wealth as it was, would sign a loan with old Ebenezer from time to time. His fortune was rumored to be ten times that of the bank. The rumor was never argued and assumed to be fact.

Still, as his mortality remained uncertain, Ebenezer refused to let go of his grasp on the town. It is well known that he, who controls the wealth, controls the community.

Ebenezer left his business practices in the capable hands of Bob Cratchit, his only employee since his business partner Jacob Marley passed away to a heart attack six years prior. Cratchit was a devoted man, willing to do anything Ebenezer requested, or demanded at times, yet knowledgeable to run the business in Ebenezer's absence. The best part about the deal was that Cratchit worked for pocket change, just enough to keep his family alive. For running the Ole' Loan Shoppe during his absence, Ebenezer gave Cratchit two extra pence for the extra hours he worked that winter.

Since his absence, and with returned vigor and health, Ebenezer expected the same hours to be worked by Cratchit, from the sun's first peek above the horizon to its demise upon the opposite. The winter months were especially hard on Cratchit and his family, leaving his wife, two daughters, and three sons to chop the firewood, stoke the fire, and tend to the repair work that winter's devastation brings forth. A hole had recently formed in the ceiling, above his sick son's bed, forcing the family to move Tiny Tim into the cramped living room, snuggled on the floor in front of the fireplace to sleep.

Tiny Tim wasn't sick with an infection or bacteria, as one might think when they hear the word sickness. Instead, he was crippled in his legs, forcing him to walk upon two carved stick that propped him up. He was thought to be weak and easily overcome with any sickness that floated in the air around him. The Cratchit family kept him boxed up in their site, rarely allowing him to venture out into the world alone, especially in the winter time. Yet, he still made his way out whenever opportunity allowed. Cratchit loved his son dearly, wishing he could stay home and fix the how in the roof, but knew that time was sparse in the winter months.

Cratchit loved his job; he was very good at it. However, the pay, or lack of it, was enough to make him leave for something less stressful, such as a teller in the bank or a cashier at the local grocer. Yet, he knew that Ebenezer would not allow him to leave; that he would threaten the businesses to raise their interest rates or refuse to allow them to borrow more money if they took on Cratchit's employment. So, Cratchit sat at his desk, stuck in the corner away from the fire's reach, and scribble down numbers in the stacks of books he used to track the loans and notate defaults.

Cratchit shivered as he looked up from his ledger, noticing the snow began to fall more steady that it was when he arrived just before 6:00 a.m. The sun was rising and a glimpse of its warmth started to remove the frost from the thin window panes. As it melted, he felt hypnotized watching the ice crystals fade away. He didn't even notice Ebenezer strolling down the walk until the bell above the front door broke the silence of the room.

"Cratchit, what in damnation are you doing staring out of that window like a love sick school girl," his gruff voice bellowed out. "I'll be damned if I will pay you for lost time. Expect a 1% deduction from your pay this week."

Cratchit jumped in his seat, "My apologies, Sir. I was just finishing with the weekly defaults and thought I would refocus my eyes before moving on to the next task. I imagine you wouldn't want my eyes seeing fuzzy numbers and confusing some of the figures."

"That may be," said Ebenezer, his brows furrowed as he shook his cane toward Cratchit. "However, losing yourself in a fantasy is no way to refocus your eyes. Why not put on a pot of coffee, not too hot, but enough to warm my bones, and I may forgive the deduction and pay you in full this week. Maybe."

"Yes Sir," said Cratchit as he jumped from his seat and rushed to the fire to prepare the coffee. "I was wondering,"

"Always wondering, you are," interrupted Ebenezer.

"Yes Sir," continued Cratchit as he prepared the coffee. "I know you are not a fan of the holidays. However, I was wondering if I might receive an increase in my salary so I might purchase a goose for my family to celebrate the Christmas season and celebrate our thanks for what little we have in this vast world."

"An increase," chuckled Ebenezer. "You see our books, how do you expect me to provide you with an increase in pay?"

It was true that Cratchit knew the books inside in out. He was the one person that knew everything about Scrooge's business, besides Scrooge himself. On paper, the business was doing better than it ever had. Profits were skyrocketing and defaults were at an all-time low.

"Sir, you are correct," Cratchit tried not to stumble upon his words. "It seems like a slight increase would be doable. Of course, I would only expect to borrow it from the following week's pay. I would not expect it to be permanent."

"Borrow, you say?" asked Ebenezer. "Well, let me think it over. But, don't expect a yes out of me."

"Yes sir, very good sir," said Cratchit as he passed a warm cup of coffee to Ebenezer.

Ebenezer took a sip, letting the warm liquid linger upon his tongue before swallowing it down and taking another sip.

"Cratchit," said Ebenezer between drinks. "Bring me the defaults; I want to schedule meetings with the low life leaches."

Cratchit rushed to his desk and pulled the default book from atop it, consciously ensuring he did not glance out the window as he did. The book was large, nearly full of names and date, alongside the numbers that represented their debt. The people in the book were often penalized by an extra payment or increased interest rate, before their property was taken out from under them, leaving them on the street to fend for themselves. Ebenezer wasn't the law of the town, but his power superseded that of the most powerful man; he who controls the wealth, controls the world.

"Here it is, Sir," said Cratchit as he handed the book to Ebenzer. He enjoyed default time more than he should, but only because he was able to spend time in front of the fireplace. "There is only one name this week, Miss Janice. She was in bed sick all week and could not stop by to bring her fees."

"No one could bring it for her?" asked Ebenezer.

"No Sir," said Cratchit. "Her son was in the next town over, trying to find work. However, Miss Janice is feeling better and said she will bring payments from last week and this week; expecting to be caught up."

"Very good," said Ebenezer. "When she arrives, I shall speak to her. Now, get back to work."

***

The sun rose high overhead, bringing unexpected warmth to the late December day. Cratchit stretched his arms as he finished registering the new loans, looking at the old grandfather clock just as is chimed the noon hour's arrival. Like clockwork, Miss Janice entered the front door, as though she waited for the grandfather clock to introduce her.

"Good afternoon Miss Janice," said Cratchit as he took her coat and hung it on the coat tree.

"Lovely day," she said, returning his graciousness.

"We need to speak, Miss Janice," said Ebenezer, his gruff voice littered with business focus. "Please, have a seat by the fire."

Cratchit returned to his desk, keeping his ear open to spy on the conversation. He knew it was not going to be pleasant, but the more prepared he was for Ebenezer's demand, the easier the remaining of his shift would be.

"Miss Janice," said Ebenezer. "I understand you have missed a loan payment. Cratchit has already explained your position, so I will forego your repetitive banter and get down to business."

"Mr. Scrooge," replied Miss Janice.

"I would beg your pardon, Miss Janice," interrupted Ebenezer. "I pray you refrain from butting in further as I attempt to speak. As I was saying, you are well aware of your loan terms. You signed your own name right here, did you not?"

"I did, but," she tried to explain.

"Of course you did. Therefore, you know that you now owe me three payments by the end of this week. I assume you only brought two, so I will give you until Friday to bring the rest."

"But that is tomorrow," she replied with tears welling in her eyes.

"So it is," said Ebenezer coldly. "We close at 8:00 p.m. tomorrow, so I will see you before then."

"But that is Christmas Eve, how could you be so cruel?" her tears started to spill down her rosy cheeks.

"Cruel?" he asked. "I am giving you well over 24 hours; I think that is more than fair. Especially since the contract clearly states it is due earlier than that. Bring me the money tomorrow, or I will be there Saturday morning to retrieve the key to your home. Good day, now. I'll see you tomorrow."

Ebenezer stood from his chair, his joints cracking as he did so. He motioned Miss Janice toward the door before disappearing into the back room where he kept his liquors. Miss Janice stood there shocked, not sure what to do next.

Cratchit grabbed her coat from the coat tree and wrapped it around her shoulders, helping her toward the door. "I'm Sorry, Miss Janice."

She knew better than to try to reason the issue with Cratchit, he was just Ebenezer's pawn, it was well known in town. She could see in his eyes that he was sorry, but also that there was nothing he could do to make things better. The tears poured from her eyes as sobs forced the cold air into her lungs as she walked out into the stoop and down the snow covered steps.

Tiny Tim sat on the bottom step, his coat wide open, allowing the winter's chill to beat upon his skin tight flesh through his tattered sweater.

"Merry Christmas, Miss Janice." He yelled out, waving at her.

"Thank you, Child," she said, hiding her face from him as she walked off toward home.

"Tiny Tim," yelled Cratchit. "What in God's name are you doing here?"

"I was bored at home and thought I'd come to town and see what was going happening," he replied.

"Come inside before you catch the death," he said. "And don't touch anything; Mr. Scrooge is not in a good mood today."

"Yes sir," said Tiny Tim as his father helped him up the steps.

***

The grandfather clock rang out at the 1:00 hour. Tiny Tim jumped as he sat in front of the fireplace, upon the plush armchair that angled toward it. Within seconds of the chime's fade, Ebenezer exited the back room and to the coffee pot, pouring himself another cup of the blackened brew. He turned toward his chair and stopped in his tracks.

"Why are you in my chair, boy?" He scolded.

"Just keeping warm, sir," said Tiny Tim. "Poppa told me to be quiet so I wouldn't disturb anything."

"He did, did he?" replied Ebenezer. "Cratchit, am I running a daycare now? Should I deduct a babysitting fee from your pay?"

"No sir," replied Cratchit as he grabbed Tiny Tim from the chair and escorted him toward the door. "He stopped by to say hi, so I thought it best he warm up before heading home. He seems warm now; I'll see that he is on his way."

"Yes, you will," said Ebenezer. "See to it that the vermin does not return. I do not need to catch sickness from that urchin."

Tiny Tim didn't pay any attention to the name calling. "Poppa, did you ask about the increase in pay? Will we be eating goose this Christmas?"

"Now is not the time," said Cratchit, pushing Tiny Tim out onto the front stoop.

"Now, why isn't this the time?" asked Ebenezer. "Well, little boy, it seems you will not be eating goose this Christmas. Someone was late on a payment this week. So, the money is not there. If your father would have thought ahead, not that I would expect such a value to be instilled within him, he would have visited the person and retrieved the payment so it was not late. Maybe, just maybe, then you might eat goose."

"How is that fair, Sir," said Tiny Tim.

"Tim," cut in his father. "Just go, I we will discuss this at home. Please, it is time to leave."

***

Tiny Tim hobbled down the steps, looking back over his shoulder, swearing under his breath at Mr. Scrooge's lack of compassion. He stood at the bottom for a few seconds contemplating what he would tell his mother when he returned home. He wasn't in a hurry, although he knew he would be missed if he stayed away too long. Still, he was too angry to return, so he decided to meander around town until his anger faded.

Looking down the Southern end of the street, he noticed a few boys playing kick the can. Since his younger days, not that he was grown by any means; he wished to play out on the streets with boys like them. However, without surgery, he knew that playing street games was out of his grasp.

Tiny Tim walked around the corner, into the alleyway next to Scrooge's loan shop. He looked upward, toward the window that shielded his father's desk from the elements, noticing his dad was not there. His mind meandered to thoughts of Ebenezer yelling at his father, probably taking away more pay from their pocket.

"Tiny Tim," said an old voice from within the shadows of the alley. "Is that you boy?"

"Yes, Sir," he replied. "Who are you?"

"Ah, let's not allow names to muddy the waters," he said with a belly laugh

"What is it you want?" asked Tiny Tim, keeping his distance from the stranger.

"Child," said the voice, still hidden within the shadows. "I saw how Ebenezer Scrooge treated Miss Janice. I also saw the way he scolded you and refused to give your father money for a Christmas goose."

"You saw that?" asked Tiny Tim.

"I did," the voice responded. "I think I can help you get that Christmas goose and help Miss Janice save her home from foreclosure."

"How?" asked Tiny Tim eagerly.

"Well, I happen to have something here that will make Mr. Scrooge face his ghosts, the invisible demons that he hides deep within with his compassion. With it, things will change around here," said the man. "But, I cannot give it to him; it has to be given in secrecy, without his knowledge.

"Can I help?" said Tiny Tim, a spark present in his voice.

"You can," said the man. "I was hoping you would."

"What can I do?" Tiny Tim stepped closer to the man, all fright in his bones shed from existence.

"Take this," said the man, his arm outreached with a brown vial clutched within. "Pour it in Mr. Scrooge's coffee, and let it do its job."

"What if he sees me?" asked Tiny Tim.

"Don't let him," replied the man. "I'll do the rest. Do what I say and you will be rewarded greatly."

"Will it hurt him?" asked Tiny Tim.

"It will kill him," said the man. "He will, face his demons, and then die."

"Why would you do that to him?" asked Tiny Tim.

"I'm not doing anything to him," replied the man. "You are. Do you want a Christmas goose, or not?"

"I do, but killing a man is a horrible sin," replied Tiny Tim.

"What about killing an entire town?" said the man. "That is what Ebenezer is doing. He and I started that loan business to help the town, all the money he has belonged to me, now look what he has done."

"You, but Jacob Marley was his partner," said Tiny Tim.

"I was, now I am dead," said Marley. "Now he needs to be dead, to bring life back to this town. Will you save the town from its demise?"

Tiny Tim grabbed the bottle from the stranger's hand. He looked it over, but there was no label to share what it was. He looked up to ask the stranger what was inside, but the man was gone.

***

"Cratchit," yelled Ebenezer. "Go to the corner shop and fetch me some soup for my lunch."

"Yes, Sir," replied Cratchit as he grabbed his coat and rushed outside. He never hesitated when Ebenezer was hungry; it wasn't worth the potential tongue lashing it would bring forth.

***

Tiny Tim rounded the corner just as his father walked off toward the corner shop. He wasted no time ascending the steps. Yet, he cracked the door open only slightly, just enough to slip his slender frame through without ringing the bells.

Once inside, Tiny Tim hobbled toward the back where the fire was, looking around to ensure Mr. Scrooge was nowhere in sight. He left his braces at the door, so they wouldn't make unnecessary noise on the wooden floor.

As he approached the fire, where the copper coffee pot rested, he could hear Mr. Scrooge humming in the back room. Not wanting to waste any time, or risk being caught, Tiny Tim removed the cork from the vial and poured the clear contents into the remaining coffee. The liquid looked like nothing more than water, but Tiny Tim didn't question its chemical makeup. Instead, he started to hobble back toward the front door.

Footsteps echoed from the back room, signaling that Mr. Scrooge was making his way out. Tiny Tim dropped to the floor and proceeded to crawl toward the front door, using the furniture to hide behind as he did so. He didn't look back until he reached the door, just in time to see Mr. Scrooge pour a large cup of coffee and chug it down before disappearing into the back room once again.

Worried that he might be caught if he remained too much longer, Tiny Tim grabbed his braces and snuck back outside. Once out on the stoop again, he could see his dad exit the shop with Ebenezer's lunch. Not wanting to wait for his father to catch him, he hid beside the steps until his father was inside the loan shop, and it was safe that he would not be caught.

***

"Cratchit," yelled Ebenezer from the back room. "Is that you?"

"Yes, Sir," he replied. "I have your soup."

"Forget the soup," said Ebenezer emerging from the back room. "I'm not feeling well, so I'm going home. You eat the soup and lock up when you leave."

"Yes, Sir," replied Cratchit. "Are you okay?"

"I'm fine," he replied. "I just need some rest. Don't skip out early, either. I'll be back tomorrow, bright and early. Have a pot of coffee ready."

Ebenezer walked lazily toward the front, grabbing his coat and hat as he approached the door. His pace was like that if a drunkard after a spending the night with the bottle. Cratchit was worried that he had suddenly taken ill, but was also relieved that the rest of his shift would be quiet. It would give him plenty of time to figure out how to tell his wife that there would be no goose for Christmas.

***

As Cratchit arrived home, his wife met him at the door with a warm hug and a kiss. Despite their lack of money and possessions, their life was wealthy with love and heart. As Cratchit caressed his wife, he peered into the house, noticing Tiny Tim sitting in front of the fire, sadness in his eyes.

"Any news on the Goose?" asked his wife.

"I think I may be able to convince him," said Cratchit, looking in at Tiny Tim. "He said not at first, but I think he warmed up to the idea throughout the day."

"Well, let's hope for a better tomorrow then," she said, planting another kiss on his cheek. "Now, let's get some hit stew before bed."

***

The morning sun rose above the horizon, shining brightly in through the window, smacking Cratchit right in the eyes. He opened them slightly before jumping from his spot and landing on his feet.

"Oh my," he exclaimed with a shaky voice. "I've overslept! Mr. Scrooge is going to cut my throat. I have to go."

Mrs. Cratchit grabbed his Mr. Cratchit's suit and helped him with his jacket. He wasted no times pulling up his pants and tying his shoes before running to the front door. As he flung the entry open, ready to run all the way to work, Mr. Banley, the banker, greeted him.

"Mr. Cratchit," he said, holding out his hand to shake. "I was hoping I'd find you here. Merry Christmas, are you enjoying your eve festivities?"

"I would love to chat, Mr. Banley," said Cratchit. " However, I must get to work before Mr. Scrooge has my head."

"Oh my," he said, shaking his head. "Have you not heard?"

"Heard what?" he replied.

"Mr. Scrooge passed away last night. He left a note at the bank, for me to find, that asked to check on him this morning and that if he was dead, he wanted us to present a goose to every family in town for Christmas."

"Oh my," said Mr. Cratchit. "That is horrible."

"Horrible?" replied Mr. Banley. "Yes, it is always horrible when someone passes away. But, I must say, this is definitely your lucky day."

"I'm sure I am not sure what you mean," said Cratchit.

"In his will, Mr. Scrooge left the business and all of his wealth to you," Mr. Banley said with a joyous tone. "Every last bit of it."

Mrs. Cratchit and the children were at the door behind him, each speechless.

"Father," said Tiny Tim. "Does this mean you can take today and Christmas off of work?"

"I think that means he can take the entire weekend off, if he'd like," said Me Banley. "Come on down to the bank on Monday, and I'll make sure all of the paperwork is in order."

Mr. Banley turned back toward town, tipping his hat goodbye. Cratchit ushered his family back inside, out from the cold. He hugged his wife, pulling Tiny Tim close to his side as well.

"Put another log on the fire, let's stay inside and enjoy the warmth, maybe plan out how we can patch that hole in the roof."

Yellow Wrapped Gift

I brought her a present. Yellow paper with a purple ribbon, just like the one that I gave her on our first date. I remember it like it was yesterday; she was the most beautiful woman in the world. She still is. I had no idea what she liked back then so I bought her a locket and placed a picture of her dog inside; I was sort of clueless when it came to girls. The man at the corner dime store said all women liked lockets because it was a way to keep memories close to their hearts, so I took his word for it and wrapped it in yellow. He was right, she loved it and wore it every day. For the last 50 years, I'd give her a yellow wrapped present on our anniversary, her birthday, and at Christmas. The familiar wrapping always seemed to pick her up, or at least put on a fake smile for a bit. A yellow wrapped present seems to be the perfect gift for today.

I'm nervous, just like that first date so many years ago. I'm wearing my best suit, the one she says made me look like a young stallion. I know it doesn't, but her words are my yellow wrapped gift. The walk to the front door is one of the longest I've ever traversed. The world around me has disappeared as I place one step in front of the other, ever so slowly as I clear my head and try to focus. There is familiarity in some of the faces that I pass by, those that disobey my determined pace, as they stop to shake my hand and whisper

Christmas merriment into my ear. I am too focused to be courteous to their salutations. I am here to be with my wife, this is her day, and I plan on focusing all of my attention only on her before the mood changes to the joyous holiday we have celebrated together for so much of our lives.

The steps leading to the door are steep, it takes me some time to reach the top as I fight through the arthritic assault that rattles my knees. The railing is a bit higher than I remember, so I have to contort my torso in a manner that I have not been able to do in a long time just to manage my own ascension. That's okay though, she is worth every ounce of soreness I might feel tomorrow and the days to come.

It's been a long time since I've been to the church; never was much of a believer in religion and all the mumbo jumbo that goes along with it, but Christmas together was always a highlight of my year. She has come here every Saturday evening and Sunday morning, and Christmas service since before her and I were even together. It feels weird being here, standing in front of the towering oak doors, but after fifty years of marriage, this seems like the perfect time to come. The doors make me more nervous, more so than when I asked her out on the second date. My old heart seems to be working overtime as I grasp the cold brass knob and pull. It is heavy and I strain to allow entry into her sanctuary. For 50 years I've only stepped in here once, on our wedding day, but today is her day and I am adamant to be at her side.

Someone from within pulls the door open. The warm air rushes out and tickles the goose bumps upon my arm, sending strange shivers down my spine. It is as though God, whoever he or she may be, is reaching out a welcome hand. It is the same feeling my wife has tried to convince me that she feels each time she enters this holy place. It is the reason why she spends so much time here; it is why she chooses to worship here.

Ornate façade mimics the opulence worthy of a king, yet the humble murmurs inside foretell acceptance despite my lack of belief. I meander toward the back, near the holy water basin and the illuminated Christmas tree, catching my breath and composing myself after the long walk and ascension of the stairs. I want to look and feel my best when I approach her, when she realizes that I finally made my way into the house of her lord. To be at her side. To see what she experienced on the nights I played poker with the guys or had a beer or two at the corner bar. We both have our escapes. Then we come home to each other, refreshed and relaxed, and start our week anew. It is our recipe for a happy marriage. That is why we have lasted so long. It is only fair I do this for her.

I close my eyes and take a deep breath. I hear the whispers of those around me. I can't tell what they are saying, but I feel their gaze upon me as their intermingled vocalizations wrap around my flesh, like a welcoming hug. It doesn't make me feel more comfortable and I know I must go forth, to her side, before someone chooses to approach me and talk. I am here for my dear love, no one else.

Present in hand, my lazy stride takes me onward down the center aisle. More whispers mingle in the silence. Their faces are blurred, like those outside, the dim light above helps to block them out. I don't know what to expect when I stop at her side and place the present in her hands.

I imagine she will be happy that I am here, I know she will be. Her happiness is my one life goal. Without her happiness, I am nothing. Without her, I am but a lost soul wandering an ocean of blackness. She has become one in my heart and that is why I'm here.

She is near the front, all alone. The candles before her cast an angelic glow upon her face. My heart skips a beat as I lay my eyes on her and a lump gathers in my throat. Her hair is pulled back and the makeup upon her face is just enough to accentuate her natural beauty. She is absolutely ravishing in the navy-blue dress she has worn at Christmas for the last ten years. It is modest, just as she prefers, but gives a sense of purpose and accomplishment to her look. She is the most beautiful creature on this Earth.

She looks tired. I am not sure if she notices

me at her side, so I reach out and place the yellow wrapped present with the purple bow in her hands. The cooled air has placed a chill upon her flesh. I wrap my shaky hands around hers, placing the small yellow present intertwined between our fingers, its bright colors contrasting against her matured flesh. In age, she has become frail, although feisty as the day we met, maybe even more so. Keeping her warm is a never-ending battle most days. Today is no exception.

As I hold her, I draw my head down and place a tender kiss upon her forehead. The familiar scent of her makeup and perfume gathers upon my lips and nose. I used to despise the taste it left behind, but over time, it has become a delicacy of sorts. A lasting reminder that she is by my side, even when we are apart. She never splurges, except for the makeup she puts upon her face and the perfume she puts upon her neck. Nothing but the best for my girl.

Standing there, by her side, I feel a hand upon my shoulder. It is the pastor, a man I have met at a few events here and there. He wants me to take a seat so the ceremony can begin. I don't want to sit. Sitting means I must remain through the whole ceremony, despite my unease and anxiety summoning in my chest. He is politely insistent though. So, I will do it for my dear love. Before sitting, though, I lean over and plant one final kiss upon her rosy pink lips. One final peck as I whisper one final *I love you. Although the yellow wrapped present may be nothing more than an empty box, the purple ribbon holds in the greatest gift I could ever give; my love for all eternity.*

With hesitance, I back away from the coffin, walking backwards to my seat. I don't want anyone to see the tears in my eyes as I let the love in my heart melt away my soul. Today I say goodbye to the love of my life on Christmas day. Not with the pomp and circumstance she deserves, not with a morbid farewell. Instead, for the last time, I say goodbye to her with a yellow wrapped present, secured with a purple ribbon.

This Little Piggy

The starry night's serenity was shattered when the large rooster crowed for the world to wake, tricked by the full moon's unusual luminescence. Repeatedly, the black feathered night demon thrust out his chest, a sign of dominance around his brood of chicks, spitting out *cock-a-doodle-doos* into the cool farm air. The other farm animals returned their dismay; mooing cows demanded quiet and the donkeys exclaimed grunty *Neighs* in disapproval of the late night antics.

Lights inside the cozy farmhouse blinded the night, revealing the waking of the residents within. Edgar, a short and burly man with a penchant for theatrics, burst from the front door, rifle in hand, yelling obscenities into the air as his wife demanded he choke the cock until it lie flaccid on the soiled ground.

"I expect that damn rooster to be on the Christmas dinner table tomorrow night, or you'll be fuckin' sleeping in the car again," she demanded.

"Fuck all that," Edgar replied. "Those animals is my babies, and Cocky Corrie is a damn fine specimen. He won me two blue ribbons at the 4-H last year and I'll be damned if I'm gonna cook him up like Jeffrey Dahmer did to his cocks."

Edgar hobbled his way toward the barn, stepping over puddles in the driveway, his short legs barely making it across without getting his shoeless feet wet, soaking his socks through to the skin.

"And I'll tell you another thing," he yelled behind him. "Don't worry about keeping my side of the bed warm, I'm sleeping out in the barn with Suey tonight. She may be a smelly pig, but she snuggles a hellluva lot better than your anorexic ass does. Keep that king size bed to yourself, I'll be hittin' the hay old school tonight."

As the terrain transitioned from muddied soil to wet grass, Edgar's awkward gait caused him to lose balance and he fell flat on his back, landing his ass right in a pile of donkey shit, left there by Miss Cindy, his prize donkey. Rather than bitch and moan more than normal, he just laid there, staring up at the stars, wondering where life went wrong, why life wasn't as simple as it was when he was younger and single, before the farm and all the animals, or before he was summoned to respond to all his wife's beckoning commands. Yet, he knew the animals where why he kept going, the true loves of his life. Especially Suey and the loving gaze she returned to him each and every day when he brought her food and massaged her back between his stubby little fingers.

"Cock-A-Doodle-Dooooooooooooooooo," roared the big black cock.

"For fucks sake, Corrie," yelled Edgar. "The wife's already on my ass, shut the fuck up and go to sleep already. Give me a damned Christmas miracle, I'll tell ya, you gonna get me in more trouble with her."

The rooster didn't seem to care as Edgar sat up, his arms propping his rotund body upright. His movements were slow and steady as he tried to stand without falling again. His eyes were still affixed upon the sky when he caught flashes of red and blue from the barn area.

"Dammit," he said to himself. "Now the police are here, fuckin' great."

He tried to stand faster, still steadying himself to ensure he didn't fall again. As he lifted his ass from the cold and damp grass, the stench of fresh donkey shit invaded his nostrils, nearly causing him to vomit right there. A nearby frog chirped from within a small patch of overgrown grass at his side as a wafting patch of fog meandered across his farm. Afraid of frogs and the fog representing a ghostly child, Edgar sprung to his feet and darted toward the barn, hoping to find solace near the police cruisers. Just as he took the first step, an explosion of light, red and blue becoming purple, filled the farm in its radiance before darting to the heavens, leaving the darkness of night behind, quiet its only companion.

"What in god's name is this fuckery?" he shouted in between heavy breaths as he jogged toward the barn, holding up his jeans with one arm, so they wouldn't fall to his knees and trip him up.

As he approached, the silence was deafening. At the gate post, where his big black cock often stood proudly, watching over his chicks, a tear trickled from his eye as the beautiful bird laid flaccid on the dirty ground, all life sucked out of him. He continued onward, not taking his eyes off of the beautiful cock until he passed by the hen house, where feathers were strewn out into the yard and splattered egg yolk littered the ramp that led up to the coop. He refused to look inside; the silence foretold what he might find, instead continuing onward into the barn.

The large oak doors were wide open, the one on the right barely hanging on by one hinge, he slowed his pace, not knowing what to expect inside. In the distance, the muffled sounds of his wife's nagging were lost in the night's odd tangle of events, but he ignored her and the bitching that erupted from her mouth.

***

Inside, scorched hay and the sweet smell of diesel filled the air as puffs of smoky haze created a veil of trickery, making it hard to see clearly. Edgar treaded carefully, hoping not to step on the carcasses of any of his beloved animals, desperately searching for Suey, hoping she was safe from harm.

He was quiet as he approached the back of the barn where Suey's dream mansion stood unscathed. The bright yellow shutters that hung upon the baby doll pink façade shone brightly amidst the smoky air. It was almost as beautiful as the day Edgar built it for the swiney love of his life.

He unclasped the latch, pulling open the middle third of the exterior door, taking a deep breath before peering inside. He closed his eyes and said a little prayer to the Christmas pork gods, hopeful she would be safe and sound inside, welcoming him with a girly grunt. To his dismay, she was nowhere to be seen inside the luxury pen. Her bed of hay remained untouched for the night; the bales he often slept on were still stacked neatly by her bed's side, even her bowl of slop remained full, untouched by her buxom snout.

"What the fuck happened here?" said Edgar out loud behind his quivering lips; the tears flowing freely. "Where's my goddamn pig!"

Without another thought, Edgar rushed out of the barn and started toward the neighbor's plot of land.

"That fuckin' piece of shit better not have been part of this," he cursed to the sky. "Shane, goddamn you, I'll rip your nuts off and feed them to Suey if you've touched her in any way that ain't natural."

As he rushed through the wet uncut grass, Edgar was stopped in his tracks as the same red and blue and purple lights ascended from behind the hilly landscape, hovering just before him. The saucer shaped craft remained still, as though it was watching him as he looked back. It taunted him, beckoning him to make another move. He was scared, trembling, unsure what to do next.

As he contemplated his plan of attack, a sliver of white light shone on the side of the craft, widening slowly as the side of the craft opened, offering a ramp that led into the bowels of the ship. Iridescent lights flicked along the sides of the ramp, alternating from the base that touched the ground and flowing upward into the craft. Edgar stood, his head cocked to the side, trying to get a closer look at what was inside.

"Well, fuck this," he said taking the first step toward the craft. "If aliens stole Suey on Christmas Eve, I ain't gonna let them get away with it. I'll fucking kick some green man ass up in here. You can choke my beautiful big black cock and smack my ass until it lies lifeless on the ground. But, if you mess with my pig, I'll take World War III to the whole universe."

***

The ramp was sturdy and was textured for plenty of traction. Although hurried, Edgar was cautious in his approach. The bright lights made it difficult to see, his squinted eyes made it more difficult to make out the complicated interior. Lining the walls were miles of fiber optic lines, each illuminated with enough data to make the entire continent of North America seem like a third world country in terms of knowledge transferred through their internet lines.

It was cold inside, like a crisp fall morning. Edgar wished he would have worn a shirt, noticing the nipples on his man boobs poking out like arrows pointing him down the corridor. Christmas in Kentucky was never this cold. Without question, he followed their directions, staring at the electronic contraptions and mangled mess of wires that decorated the interior walls. He knew nothing about what anything was, so he tried not to focus on any of it, instead hell bent on getting his pig back before she became victim to an anal probe experiment.

As he continued onward, the hallway led to a silver door. Like a science fiction movie, Edgar thought it would simply open as he approached. He was surprised when he ran right into the heavy metal door, smashing his nose into the cold barrier.

"For Fuck's sake," he yelled. "Suey gets taken by aliens that don't even have the technology for doors to open on their own? The damn grocery store can do it, why can't they?"

Edgar felt around the edges of the door, finding a small alcove near the floor that he could stick his fingers in and pull the door open. He just shook his head and continued to open the door, revealing a circular room with a large object in the middle. Confused as to what the area might be, Edgar rushed in and frantically stomped toward the object. He was blind to the rest of the room, unaware of the hundred eyes staring at him from the walls until ten large creatures blocked his path, grunting demands to stay back, while others rushed him from behind, knocking him to his knees.

"What the fuck?" he yelled. "If this ain't a bad dream, I don't know what it is."

Surrounding Edgar was a sounder of massive swine, each dark grey in color and standing on their hind legs, opposable thumbs allowing them to grasp the glowing spears in their hand that pointed nefariously toward Edgar's head and chest.

Edgar was in shock, he had no clue what to do next, so he just sat there on his knees, thinking of the worst possible scenario, clinching his ass cheeks as hard as he possible could. His eyes surveyed the room, looking for a way out, not knowing if they were still hovering over the hill outside or somewhere up in space where no one could hear his shouts for help.

As he sat there, the pillar in the middle of the room spun around. A seat at the base rotated into view with a soft whirling sound. He closed his eyes tightly, anticipating something horrible as the alien swine before him lined up in military fashion, flanking his side, standing to attention. The room was silent for a moment until a familiar grunt erupted into the air. *Suey*, he said in his head, opening his eyes, ready to fight for her life.

To his surprise, Suey sat, perched, within a throne like seat, starting back at him with a smile upon her face. She extended her arms and beckoned him forth. Edgar remained seated, looking at the alien swine at his side, wondering if he should rush to her arms.

"Fuck it," he said as he rose to his feet and ran to his sweet swine. His naked torso smashed against her warm flesh, her rows of nipples tickling his stomach as he embraced her tightly, not wanting to let go.

"Don't be frightened," said Suey in a robotic human voice.

Edgar pulled away, his jaw agape and eyes wide open, "you can talk?"

"In your language only when I wear this translator," she said with a smile. "I wanted to welcome you aboard and say thank you for rescuing me two years ago. You were the nicest human I've ever met. For a time, I thought I'd be chopped to pieces and served for breakfast. But, you found me and treated me like a queen, without knowing I actually am a queen."

"Goddamn, this is unreal," said Edgar. "I don't know what to say or think. This is a Christmas miracle!"

"Just say you'll come back with me to my planet, reign by my side as my king, and protect me always," she said, holding his hands within her own.

"I'd leave the world behind to be at your side," he said, tears spilling from his eyes as though he had just been proposed to. "You've been my queen since we met."

"Then we shall leave now," she said.

The space craft whirled as the mechanical motors burst to life, readying the ship to ascend into the heaven's, away from the Earth's gravitational pull. A feeling of weightlessness crept through the large room and Edgar's heavy frame relieved his knees from the strain they had so long been victim to. Upon a large screen a series of shapes flashed in one second intervals, an obvious countdown.

As the thrusters roared to life, Edgar knew the time was near for him to become a king, no longer a slave to his wife's nagging demands, finally sitting as equals alongside the true love of his life. His heart beat with intense palpitations as he awaited his new life, somewhat relieved that there were no anal probes involved.

As the craft was about to take off, unexpected turbulence caused the ship to shake violently, sending the alien swine scattering to battle stations, ready to fight back whatever foe might be attacking them.

"Put it on the screen," demanded Suey.

The large wall before her revealed the outside of the craft. Just below them, Edgar's neighbor Shane stood in attack mode with an elephant rifle in his hands, shooting at the space craft. His words were undecipherable among the chaos inside the ship.

"That piece of shit," said Edgar.

"Now, we must leave now!" yelled Suey.

The ship roared to life as it began its ascension toward the sky, but not before Shane let off one final shot, disrupting the craft's rotation as it shot upward. Inside, swine, Edgar, and Suey, tumbled across the floor as the inside of the ship spun out of control, while the outside remained still; opposite of how the ship should perform. Suey yelled out instructions to her crew, each working diligently to correct the abnormal functions.

The space craft zig zagged through the air, away from Edgar's farm, across the continent of North America at a speed never before traveled by Edgar. The internal structure of the craft still spun, chaotically, as the swine crew worked diligently to resolve the issue. Edgar and Suey held hands, staring into each other's eyes as they made their way to the outer hallway where they could brace themselves against the walls and be safer than inside the large internal room.

As they clutched the walls, holding tightly onto a warm pipe, Suey extended her lips toward Edgar's and they embraced each other in a passionate kiss. The hairs on Edgar's back stood erect as tingles of electric current flowed through his nerves. At last, he was with his true love.

As they kissed each other, the ship roared to life, correcting the maladaptive rotation with a sudden jolt. The entry hatch at the end of the hall thrust open wide, revealing the land below. Tilted at an angle, the ship's hallway became a slide upon which Suey's massive body descended upon. Edgar tried to hold her, but his fingers slipped upon her naked flesh; he watched her horrified expression as she slipped outside, crashing to the land below, as the ship thrust upward into the heavens and the hatch shut tightly closed. Tears ran down his face as he yelled out sobbing promises to find her and bring her home.

***

A small farm in Wisconsin was brought to life as red and blue lights filled the night sky for a full two minutes. The childless inhabitants were woken from their slumber, rushing outside to see what disrupted their sleep.

As they opened the front door, a strange ship sped out of view, rising upward faster than anything they had ever witnessed. The young couple glanced at each other, in disbelief, neither saying a word about the alien space ship they just witnessed, instead running to the field where it was hovering.

"What is that, Sus," said her husband.

"Not sure, John," she replied. "But, it is moving."

Both ran to the creature that lay on the ground, barely moving, but obviously alive. It was pig-like in shape, but with opposable thumbs and an almost human face.

"Is this an alien?" asked john, in disbelief.

"What else could it be," said Sus.

"Are you thinking what I'm thinking?" said John.

"I am," said Sus. "Grab its legs."

***

Inside the small farmhouse, John and Sus carried the alien pig down a set of dusty stairs, into a musty old basement. Toward the back, John shuffled the weight of the pig as he freed a hand to unlock a heavy door toward the back. The pig's weight made it awkward to get the door open, but with some fumbling he was able to reach success.

Inside, John hit the light switch with his shoulder, illuminating the room, revealing plastic lined walls, a strange swing hanging in the corner of the room, a surgical grade table lined with an assortment of sexual toys, and many more oddities that are rarely seen in the presence of such openly religious churchgoers as Sus and John.

"If only the town knew how kinky we are," said John with a giggle.

"Right?" replied Sus. "Can you imagine if Miss Johnson knew I spent Sunday evenings in here with you shoving that double dong in my ass while taking the lord's name in vein?"

Both laughed uncontrollably until there were tears, while propping the alien pig up against the South wall. Chains and handcuffs lined the concrete wall, hanging low enough to secure the pig into place, leaving her little room to move. John, worried her squeal might be noticeable, grabbed a well-worn red ball gag from the table and affixed it to the alien pig's mouth.

"I reckon she'll wake soon," said John. Let's head upstairs and let her acclimate to the new surroundings before we start in on her."

"Yeah, you're probably right. Besides, you have to be up early to give the sermon at church. Christmas day sermons are always so drawn out and boring, but at least we have something to look forward to when we get home," said Sus.

"I can't wait," said John, giving Sus a peck on the cheek. "Maybe we'll show this alien pig what an anal probe is, human style."

"Merry Christmas, Baby," said Sus to John, returning the kiss on his cheek.

"Merry Christmas," he replied. "This will be the best on ever."

Black Cats and Santa Hats

Upon the frosty winds of Christmas, Santa's sleigh sailed the sky from home to home to leaving presents for all the good boys and girls. Squeezing down chimneys sliding under apartment doors, the jolly old elf let no barrier deny his entry to provide joy on his favorite day. His visits were swift and his departures were hasty as the journey's demands required alacrity.

Within the gentle snowfall over the United States Midwest, Old Saint Nick approached a single-story ranch to check off three more names from upon his list. He squeezed his body down the chimney and wriggled through the hearth, quiet as a mute mouse as he wiped the soot from his beard. Flanking the brick and mortar fireplace, fragrant candles greeted his advent with aromas of cinnamon and pine.

Three stockings upon the mantle matched the names upon his list; Odin, Luna, and Artemis. From within his sack he retrieved some stuffers, sliding them in the ornate socks. Their shaken contents echoing through the night, he grasped the stockings to silence the clatter before tip-toeing toward the dimly lit tree where presents he would leave. From within his sack glorious boxes emerged, shimmering and shining festive wrapped. Their movement reflected the brilliance of the lights, casting illuminated points upon the wall. The disco display dances around as Santa emptied his sack, leaving the Christmas man unaware of what appeared behind his back.

Within the shadowed spaces around, two sets of yellow and one pair of green eyes dilated wide upon cat faces. The pirouetting luminosities captured curiosity as the feline demons fell into trance. Without warning, they dove forth, tripping Santa to the floor. The jostled packages shone brighter as they tumbled to and fro. Luna Bean, the female cat, scratched at the lights upon Santa's face. Her razor claws cut deep within his saintly flesh, releasing blood of a demigod. Her brother Odin, a beefy black mouser joined in on the holiday fun. He dove upon the fat man's pulsating chest, knocking the breath right out of him. Grasping for air and weary from the fall, Santa twisted his body to rise to his feet, exhausting the energy within. He removed his hat and smacked the cats, sending them running frantic. However, his assault was not unseen as the green-eyed tuxedo lurked close by. Although clawless and feeble, the rescued feline stalked with demented inquisitiveness as he swooped from the darkness, grabbing the Santa hat within his teeth, running behind the Christmas tree.

Santa cursed the most unspeakable word and demanded the trio return his cap. His words were ignored as the three climbed in the tree, knocking it over onto the welcomed intruder. An exposed wire within the stringed lights tickled electricity upon Santa's nose. Expletives shouted as the shock stung deep and Santa threw the tree off of him. He tore from the faux display a steel corded branch and smacked the three kitties away. They hissed and they squealed as the metal met fur, their anger filled with hate. The trio of cats demanded his leave, their motions backing him to the hearth. He held out his hands and beckoned them back, fearful of their next attack.

Rear to the fireplace, Santa begged for forgiveness and asked for his sacred hat back. Arched backs and exposed fangs, the furious felines demanded the old man take leave. Artemis still holding the hat in his mouth, Luna and Odin sliced at it with claws, tearing shreds of ancient fur from its lining. The hat left in pieces, each backed away, warning of further peril if Saint Nick would not leave.

Santa took heed and motioned his surrender as he bent on one knee to retrieve his hat. He backed up quite slowly and wiggled his nose, disappearing up onto the roof, but not before the felines slashed at his suit, tearing away at the protection and comfort it bestowed.

Awaiting his return, a miniscule elf reminded of the schedule they must keep. A moment of silence and a look up and down, the elven chauffer returned Santa's unjolly frown, tilting his head in inquisitive query.

As Santa removed his tattered suit and replaced it with a spare from under his seat, while wiping warm blood away from his cheeks, he took a deep breath and looked back at the chimney where whispering meows warned it was his time to go. He jumped in his sleigh and grabbed hold of the reigns, flying off into the night under the moon's mystic glow.

"Dear Lyles, my elf, a house I've never feared as delivery of joy is my most prized act. But a reminder I'll need in a house of pets to never defend from black cats with a thrashing from Santa hats."

Sins of the Diner

Nestled near the edge of a small Indiana town, close to the spot where high school kids sneak off to and make out, Duke's Diner catered to those escaping the worries of life and the prying eyes of over churched town's folk. On a Friday and Saturday nights, lonely cars and trucks filled the dirt parking lot, revving their engines under the neon lights. Teenage girls flirted, pulling up their poodle skirts above the knees, torturing the imagination of the boys that craved the fuzzy playground underneath. Of course the boys were just as flirtatious with their cars, subliminally suggesting the power under the hood was a sincere representation of the small block in their pants.

Needless to say, Duke's Diner was not a spiritual place, not even during Christmas time when television adverts transitioned to messages of goodwill toward mankind. During the week, although the jukebox still played the hits, the clientele was less rambunctious as the pop and country tunes were replaced by silent nights and jingling bells. Sitting alone at the counter, lonely recluses sipped on coffee and ate apple pie, while a few of the booths accommodated older couples hiding past sins while sharing a greasy burger, or devious businessmen dressed to capitalize on some poor unsuspecting resident. Really, it was not much different than any other small town diner on a lonely Christmas Eve.

From the kitchen, Duke yelled out the order for table 6, gesticulating that it was ready to serve. Mindy, freshly dropped out of high school and no ambitions to pursue since funds for beauty college seemed out of reach, uttered a couple indistinguishable words under her breath as she grabbed the greasy plate of burgers and fries. At only 17, she had already mastered the screw it all attitude rivaling even the most seasoned Soup Jockeys.

As she passed by the double glass doors, framed in stainless steel, a tall man in a suit entered. She faked a grimace while walking past toward her destination. He did not return the welcome, as he placed his worn briefcase on the nearest open booth table. Before sitting he looked around the room. Seven people, including Duke, occupied the diner. None but Mindy acknowledged his

121

presence as he shook his head and wiped some snow dust from his jet black wool suit before sitting down.

"Anyone ever tell ya' it's rude to wear a hat inside?" asked Mindy as she stood at the end of his booth, order pad in hand.

The man nudged his briefcase towards the back of the table and looked up at her. His dark eyes stared directly into her electric blue irises, as though searching for the source of rudeness. Her glare back at him told her entire story. Instead of prolonging her wait, he simply asked her the date, including the year.

"June 6, 51" She said with a sigh.

"Six, six, fifty-one, how fitting" he replied.

"So, cup of joe?"

"That will be fine, black please" he said, his words fading as she walked away.

Mindy turned towards the front counter to grab the stranger his cup of coffee. Frankie, an older man that frequented the stool near the coffee pot asked her who the stranger was. She simply replied that she didn't know but he kind of creeped her out.

"I can't figure out if he is a Bull or an actor, but if you need him to cut out, just let me know. I'll show him the door" said Frankie.

"Relax, he looks official, I bet he is just cruising through. I mean, look at the briefcase. It looks like the real deal."

"Probably a government official," said Frankie, sipping on his coffee. "Looking to start some trouble around here, no doubt."

"Frankie," laughed Mindy. "You think a government official is gonna take time out of spending Christmas Eve with family and come here to this greasy old diner to start some trouble in our little town? Come on. He's probably just a businessman taking advantage of the low traffic to get to his next sales call."

"Maybe," said Frankie. "But if he's doing that, then he don't care about nothing but money. Ain't no reason to trust a man like that."

"I'll be fine," she said, placing the carafe back on the coffee maker.

As the two chit-chatted, turned to deliver the coffee when the stranger stood up and asked everyone to pay attention. He had a product that he would like each person to try for free, in exchange only for word of mouth.

"See," said Frankie, groaning, recognizing the lame sales technique that he'd used when he dabbled in sales and was still green. "He ain't nothing but salesman scum, trying to take advantage of us small town folk on Christmas Eve. Trying to make a quick buck before he heads out of town."

As with everyone else in the diner, Frankie was intrigued by the man's boldness and who knew, maybe there was an idea or product he could steal for their own gain. After all, he figured, although he'd left the business long ago, sales were still in his heart.

"Ladies and gentlemen, I have here a hand cream that will smooth the day's sins from your hands, leaving them pure as the rains from Heaven and the fires of Hell."

His voice was powerful and filled with the confidence of a Baptist pastor. One of the older businessmen hiding from his family on the holiday's eve leaned to the other, whispering that he liked his style. The mysterious salesman saw the brief exchange and presented the table of suits with a small tube of lotion each. He then proceeded to pass out a sample to each of the other patrons.

"Now, before you give this miracle crème a try, I want to remind you to share your experience here today with anyone you meet. After all, word of mouth is the best advertisement."

Without further fluff, the Salesmen instructed each to apply a generous amount of product to their hands and then place their palms firmly onto the table in front of them so he could properly demonstrate the power of the potion in their hands. Each did as they were instructed, each wondering what this miracle lotion would do to their skin. It didn't take long for a slight burning sensation to spread throughout their hands and fingers.

"What the hell is this stuff, it burns!" yelled the older businessman. "My hand, it is stuck to the table, what kind of cream is this!"

"Stuck?" asked the salesman. "Oh, I'm sorry; I must have mistaken my inventory; packed the wrong product. What I gave you is a brand new creation that is called super glue. I truly am sorry for the mistake, I'm afraid you might be stuck here for quite a while."

"God damn it" yelled the younger businessman. I have to be home soon to spend time with my wife and kids to open presents before the entire family arrives tomorrow, and you are saying I'm stuck here?"

Frankie was just as vocal, threatening to show the salesman his weathered fists and bloody up his face. Duke yelled that he had food on the stove that would surely burn if he did not remove it soon. The old couple sat silently, not wanting to cause more commotion that there already was.

Despite the dark cloud that hung over the situation, Mindy simply acknowledged that the super glue would be a fantastic product since it obviously worked so well on their hands. "Hell," she said, "I bet you could glue an elephant to a tree with this stuff".

The stranger smiled at Mindy's comment and patted her on the head. "That's the spirit, young lady. See, you get it, don't you?"

His presence frightened her, especially with everyone's hands glued to the tables. She figured he would rob them all of their hard earned money, maybe rough some up a bit if they fought back. So, she decided to play it safe and kiss up to the man, hoping he would focus on others instead.

The Salesman paced the floor, eyeing each patron with a subtle intensity. He stopped at each table, and counter, taking a moment to stare deep into their eyes. The businessmen were visibly anxious as sweat dripped form the brows. Frankie and Duke both turned their heads away, deflecting his gaze. The older couple hung their heads, as though in shame. He continued to pace the room, walking past Mindy during his observations. All the while, the juke box played *God Rest You Merry, Gentlemen* in the background.

"I have a confession" said the stranger, his words spilling like sins in a confessional. "I came here today, not to sell you this new product, but confront you about the wrongdoings you have all hidden within your sinful souls."

Frankie spoke up, "I ain't got any sin to hide. All the wrong I've done is known to everyone in this damn town."

The stranger walked over to his bar stool, and sat down next to him. "I'm afraid that is a lie, Franklin. I saw what you did to poor Mr. and Mrs. Kramer's crops."

The old couple looked up from their laps, Mr. Kramer glaring at Frankie, "What did you do to my wheat Frankie."

"I didn't do nothing" replied Frankie.

"Now Frankie, it is not polite to lie to your elders. You sprayed poison on their wheat, instead of the fertilizer you told them you were spraying. Now, the entire town is eating bread made from that wheat. You don't even care that people are getting sick from it, do you" said the stranger.

"God damn it! He's lying! You can't believe this man; he ain't never even been here before." replied Frankie.

Mr. Kramer's face flushed with red. He had been confronted about the emerging sicknesses, and was being blamed for a bad crop. He was on the verge of losing everything that him and his wife had worked for. Their reputation was close to being destroyed and they were being hassled by the cops so much, they were close to packing up and leaving town. If he could have, he would punch Frankie straight in the kisser, but the glued hands prevented him from doing so.

Frankie tried to argue his innocence, but no one would listen to him. Instead the Kramer's yelled back, and Duke was furious that he was serving that same bread to his customers. The stranger grew tired of the bickering, and stood close to Frankie. Whispering something in his ear, he grabbed both sides of his head and twisted. In an instant, the swift crack of Frankie's neck released him from his life. His head flopped as the body fell to the floor, the weight of his body ripped his hands from the counter, leaving behind a fleshy print.

Mindy gasped as she began to cry, old man Kramer told his wife Martha to look away. Duke and the businessmen didn't seem to care much that Frankie was gone. He wasn't the most liked person in town anyway.

"Thanks' for doing what all of us have wanted to do for a long time" said Duke. "Now his blood is on your hands, not ours."

"Duke, you are not exactly innocent either, now are you" said the stranger.

"I guess not, sometimes I cook meat that is a day or two past its expiration, you gonna kill me too?"

"I'm talking about the side business you have going on with the town's youth. You know, the drugs you poison their brains with for a hefty profit?" the stranger twisted his lips to an evil grin.

Duke stood silently. It was no real secret; he had sold marijuana to the Kramer's to help ease their farm-life aches and pains. He even sold a little coke to the business men to keep them alert when deadlines had to be met. He was a fairly well respected entrepreneur in the town, and knew no one would dare rat him out, so he felt safe.

"I get a feeling that you have not poisoned your body with the drugs you sell, yet have no problem doing it to others. Well, this superglue stuff has some pretty toxic fumes if inhaled. How about I give you the ultimate high?" said the stranger.

Without saying another word, the stranger grabbed a fresh tube of the glue and spread a glob of it upon Duke's lips, holding them tightly together to mask his screams. Once the fast acting mixture took hold, he did the same for each nostril. The fumes permeated within Duke's head, numbing the pain of not being able to breathe through the sealed orifices. The others in the room stared speechless as Duke struggled to free himself and his reddish skin turned to a deep purple. Within a few minutes his body became limp and fell to the floor on the opposite side of the counter to Frankie. The same fleshy handprints remained on the counter.

Mindy and Mrs. Kramer both sobbed uncontrollably, scared for their lives. The men did not say a word, hoping to avoid the attention it would bring forth. However, each knew deep down that their sins were just as bad as those that were punished before their eyes. They hoped that their punishments were less severe that those already given out.

The stranger readjusted his suit coat strolled over to the businessmen. The room had become eerily quiet as the juke box stopped playing its tunes. The heavy breathes of the balding business man were almost deafening in the silence. The stranger sat next to him in the booth, and placed his hands on top of the business man's.

"Stephen, I know of your past sins, and that you have worked hard to change your ways." said the stranger. "I know you look up to Mr. Harlen here next to me, but he is a bad man. He will only guide you back to the life of greed you once led.

You want to forget about the young woman you raped when you were just a teen, and maybe you have. But I cannot forget such a nefarious deed."

Between the two sets of hands, an intense red glow illuminated. Every second it grew more intense until Stephen's entire body became awash in flames. He did not scream, nor did he fight the assault. He sat there and took the punishment like a man. When the flames died out, his corpse was gone, as though escorted to Hell by the consummation of conflagrations.

The stranger turned his head towards Mr. Harlen, who in turn looked away in an attempt to hide the tears that ran down his cheeks. He knew that his punishment would not be as gentle as those before him. He had sinned since he was little, and had no feelings of remorse. If this stranger was the devil, then he was going home.

"Robert. May I call you Robert" the question was not meant to be answered, "You are aware of your many sins, and I simply do not have time to list them all off. However, I think the Kramer's should know that you are the one that paid Frankie to poison the crops."

"Why would you do such an awful thing" shouted Mrs. Kramer. "Forget all the grief we have been put through, what about those that got sick?"

"Mrs. Kramer, he wanted your land and you would not sell. It is a classic story. The greedy man wants the farmer's land. The farmer will not sell, so he cheats and lies his way to obtaining the deed," said the stranger.

The stranger looked over to Robert and patted him on the shoulder, then got up and walked over to the older couple. He sat down and smiled genuinely while staring into their eyes. Although he has no remorse, they were the least threat to any other person in town, yet they lived a life long sin.

"You two have done nothing but good deeds for this god-fearing community. You give to the needy and you go to church every Sunday. Most would think that you have paved your path to heaven with ease. If only that were true…,"

Mindy looked onward as both Mr. and Mrs. Kramer began to sob. She always looked up to them, wishing her future would mirror their love and friendship. She wondered, if the couple was damned, what her punishment would be. Surely, they were more innocent that she was.

"Please" said Mr. Kramer," we never meant any harm. We only wanted to be together".

"You two have not only committed horrible acts of sodomy, but you have done so while in an incestuous relationship. I cannot let a brother and sister, such as you, that have committed such ungodly deeds go unpunished."

Mindy could not believe her ears. Never had she imagined that the two were blood related. Mr. Harlen fought back a glob of vomit that gathered in his throat. Never in his life would he think of even kissing his sister, if he had one.

"For your sins, I will sentence you to an eternity in purgatory, where you will relive the most horrible experiences of your life, over and over again." said the stranger. "Now, be gone with you, your father is waiting your arrival."

In a flash, the couple was gone. The stranger then turned his attention to Mr. Harlen. He approached at a slow pace, staring him down the entire length of the stroll. Mr. Harlen tried hard to look away, but could not escape the vengeful gaze. He tried to speak, to plead his case, but words would not form. The sweat on his brow began to collect in his eyes, burning and blurring his vision.

"Robert," said the stranger. "You sir, are a despicable man. Although that nice couple has sinned their way into purgatory, their misdeeds are nothing compared to yours. So, since your last act of evil was towards them, I feel it is only fair that you spend eternity feeling guilt in their presence. You sir, are going to purgatory as well. Where that couple will gain a reprieve from their torture for thirteen hours each day, and redirect their pain unto you."

In another flash, Mr. Harlen was gone. The stranger walked back to the table where the briefcase still sat. He fastened the leather straps and placed his hat back upon his head, adjusting the brim with his pasty white fingers.

He seemed unaware that Mindy remained. Her body was shivering uncontrollably, not from cold – but fear. She hoped he had forgotten about her, but wondered if it was a trick. She decided to remain quiet and stay low to the table that she sat at.

Mr. Harlan approached the front door, pushing it open. He stopped and turned towards Mindy and smiled.

"Fear not, young lady. I am not going to hurt you. You may have a bad attitude, but that is only due to the horrible life you live. Your mind is too pure to face my wrath; I can see an act like yours from a mile away."

Mindy felt the fear fade from her body, replaced with relief.

"Sir, are you Satan?"

"No" said the stranger with a laugh. "You have mistaken me for the wrong God"

With those final words, he exited the diner. As the doors shut, a momentary flash filled the room, removing the corpses that remained. Mindy cupped her face with her hands, not even realizing that she was unstuck. She took a deep breath, filling her nostrils with the sweet smell of poinsettia flowers as the Juke Box kicked back on and *Silent Night* filled the air.

White Out

Darkness displaces winter's nuclear assault as daylight anticipates emergence. Silence carries its weight upon the wipers of the wind, hiding within the snowfall's ominous twinkle. Beauty is in the air and as I step outside to shovel the walkway and warm my car, I can't help but bask in it.

A sputtered start fights against the cold. The woken belts squeal in displeasure as the heat battles Mother Nature's breathe to warm the driver's seat. I scrape away a layer of snow and a layer of ice beneath. My fingertips throb, alternating between numbness and pain, but I battle on.

I breathe in the frosty air and long to climb back in bed under the covers, dreading the fifty-mile drive into work. The day has barely begun and I already hate the path that has been set into motion. I stare up at the snow dotted sky just as a brisk wind infiltrates through all the loose fitting parts of my clothing. I curse Mother Nature and her horrid sense of wintry humor. The wind deteriorates from existence and I enter my car, now toasty warm inside as the shivers fade.

Without a second thought, I begin my journey at a snail's pace toward the highway. The entrance ramp is covered in nature's dandruff and I grasp the steering wheel tightly as I enter a frigid hell.

Despite a slow and slippery drive, all seems well along the mostly deserted highway. The lanes are clearly marked by fading tire tracks of previous adventurer's that made their way to work. Few slide offs and police lights scatter the rumble strips near the grass line, as confidence in my journey loosens my grip from the steering wheel. I whisper a *"fuck you mother nature"* under my breath and continue onward.

For twenty miles, the drive is smooth, albeit slow. I relax and enjoy the quiet ride. The snow is beautiful, I will admit, but it is also a bitch to drive in. I continue onward, anxious to finish the day and start the holiday break that follows.

Nearing twenty-five miles into my fifty-mile drive, Mother Nature reminds me that I called her a bitch and returns the insult as the blackened sky turns the darkest shade of white I have ever seen. Visibility reaches only as far as the headlights begin and the road disappears before me. I grasp the wheel and pray for relief, but mommy is pissed off.

I contemplate taking the next exit ramp and returning home, but the exits are not visible, so I continue onward. Visibility comes in just small spurts as the white out conditions refuse to lift completely. At times, I find I am in a completely different lane when the road does become visible. I am scared to death.

I apologize to Mother Nature, but she does not care.

At times, a random semi-truck or car will speed past me, not caring for other life on the road, kicking up more snow and slush, making the zero visibility a negative 20, to match the outside temperature. I wonder if they might be spirits of accidents past or if they are simply uncaring bastards on the side of Mother Nature.

The trip that typically takes me about an hour becomes nearly twice as long as the highway comes to an end, allowing me to turn right toward my final destination. My muscles shiver in nervous fear as I wonder how I survived the hellish drive. I try not to think of the journey home, I am too scared.

The parking lot is nearly empty, it seems most of the employees were much smarter than I, staying home where safety was their friend. I sit in my warm car for a few minutes, composing myself.

Just before opening my door, I notice that the sun has made an appearance, hidden behind snow clouds and the confetti curtain that falls around me.

The ground shakes beneath my feet as I struggle to remain upright. The world goes black and pain surges through my every nerve. Warmth spills across my face, crackling bones signal injury. I open my eyes. Dreams at the wheel destroy my day. White pillows surround my car, caressing me in brutal embrace.

In the ditch, below the highway, I curse falling asleep at the wheel and the dreams of safe arrival. Pain surges and damnation beckons. I am

broken. I am cold. I cannot move.

Fuck you, Mother Nature. Fuck you.

The Fool's Journey

The winter night's interlude demanded justice from the city's never ending symphony of car horns, miscreant chatter, and desire of monetary gain in many shapes and forms. For the street's minions, it was a bittersweet song of hope and regret, sanctioned by the divine disciples of damnation and greed as the hustle of life continued despite the holy holiday's arrival. Such is the life in the big city for those with the will and means to dabble in gluttonous hobbies.

For the street rats that scavenged the inner alleyways, the city was nothing more than a neglected bastion of discarded dinners and meager accommodations under the fluorescent glow of forgotten doorway lights. The nights were cold, not just during winter, but amidst the summer's blistering heat as well; cold like a shoulder of a distinguished gentleman toward that of a damned mongoloid, fearful of association by eye contact. Profitable times were barren and bleak for those that lived upon the streets, as such it had always been. The holiday retained no meaning other than the reminder that rough times were here to stay.

For the man crouched in the alleyway behind the fortune teller's shop, worry of the next day's meal and compassion from others was a day by day battle not worth the stress of night's frigid caress. He managed the last cup of burnt coffee from the nearby barista in lieu of its disposal into the nearby drain, resulting in a peaceful moment of reflection and contemplation under the washed out stars and concealed quite, caressed by the city's inner glow. Devoid of knowledge beyond his inner mind, the man sat with his back against the masonry wall, legs crossed upon the damp asphalt floor, visited by the random vermin that scurried nearby.

All in all, it was a good night.

An unexpected breeze tossed the morning's paper upon the air, sending it soaring on an updraft toward the sky. He used to wish for the freedom to soar, until he realized the wind was the true master that determined the course. One to defy the nature of authority's dictatorship, the man chose to wander the city and create his own future where destiny twisted at his beck and call. Despite his fire and brimstone upbringing, he chose to leave the deities behind and discover the meaning of life on his own. Although there were times he longed to rejoin the gospel and share his journey with all that dared listen, he understood that would mean he would be stuck in the chains of religion once again, with no plan of escape as he sat upon the golden throne of revival. Christmas time was always a tough reminder of what could have been compared to what was.

Lost in thought, the rusted metal door beside him creaked open with caution, the light from within washing out the figure that exited. She was quite noisy as she propped the door open with a nearby brick, dragging it across the ground in a steady motion. She struggled with the bag of garbage in her hand, working hard to keep it from scraping against the jagged bricks and tearing open. Litter that marked the sides of the alley exposed she was not always successful.

A man of compassion, the homeless wanderer stood within his spot and cleared his throat to signal his presence, determined not to frighten the old woman. His introduction caught her attention as she stared him up and down. He smiled the best he could between his chapped and cracked lips, offering his hand without advancing forward. Apprehensive at first, the woman dropped the bag a foot in front of her and the man picked it up. Without an exchange of words, he carried it to the nearby dumpster. The bag was heavy and filled with clattering bottles and the sloshing of sauces. He was careful to handle the bag with respect, concerned it would tear open and litter the surroundings.

With his back turned, the light from the door faded to a sliver and disappeared altogether with a banging smack as the woman allowed the door to slam shut behind her upon reentry of the shop. The man did not let the dismissal of her presence bother him; he was accustomed to such acts when he attempted kindness upon others. If he were a lesser man, he might have dropped the bag upon the ground and flashed a finger in her direction, but he knew he was better than that.

As the dumpster lid smashed downward onto the metal casing, he wandered over to the spot he was seated upon and crouched to retrieve his canvas duffle bag and half empty cup of coffee. The bones in his knees cracked as his grunts echoed upon the alley's walls. Although not quite middle aged, he often felt he was on the downward slope of age's hill.

Standing back up was a tedious chore. The heavy duffle forced him lopsided as he tried to keep balanced upon his feet. Using the building's wall as support, he managed to right himself in preparation of moving onward to another alleyway in which he could hide his presence and welcome slumber until the morning's light molested his eyes to face the day.

Within a few steps toward the bustling street, the creaking door signaled its opening once again. The man stopped and as the light cast its glow upon the ground, spreading his shadow onward toward the sidewalk in front of him. He did not turn his body, opting to twist his neck to the woman's direction.

"What is your name, sir?" the old lady's voice was filled with curiosity and highlighted with the crackling rasp of a smoker.

"Ma'am, it's been so long that anyone has asked, I can't honestly say I remember," he responded with his head hung to the ground. "Mostly, I just go by *the fool.*"

"The Fool, you say," she said with her head cocked to the side. "Come closer; let me take a look at you in the light."

The Fool was apprehensive, but abided by her command. He took short steps and kept his head hung, not in shame but in respect for her age and wisdom. Not wanting to seem as a threat, he stopped a couple steps short of her position, unsure of how the woman would react to his requested approach.

"Give me your hand, let me see your story," she said when he stopped.

The Fool extended his free hand after adjusting the duffel bag upon his shoulder. His back contorted to the left upon its weight. He held it toward her with his palm facing the heavens and fingers spread wide. His head still hung low, he averted his eyes to see what the woman was doing as she grabbed his hand and traced the creases throughout his palm, twirling her digit upon his flesh. It felt odd to feel the touch of another, especially one so caring and gentle.

"Ah, I see now," she said letting go of his hand and crossed her arms over her breasts. "You are a fool, so filled with potential and a heart of gold. I see that someday you will achieve greatness, but not until the time is right within the stars."

"Ma'am, greatness is not something I wish for," he said. "I am content with the smile upon your face and the acknowledgement of my presence."

"As is your way," she responded with a smile upon the sides of her lips. "For your generosity, I want to present you with a small gift that represents my gratitude and a journey that may end in small reward, if completed without the interfering hindrance of the major arcana."

The Fool was not sure how to respond to the woman as she reached deep into a pocket within her shawl and pulled out a single tarot card. She presented it to him face down in her palm before turning it upright and extending it toward him and placing it in his still open hand.

"Thank you," he managed to stutter out.

He held the card in his hand, realizing it was the fool from the tarot deck. He never dabbled in such mystical devices in the past, a leftover stigma from his days of religion. Somehow the card felt right against his flesh, giving meaning to his street name.

"What does it mean?" he asked with his head cocked to the side.

"Sir, as a diviner and a soothsayer, I can say that you already know the meaning of that card; you just don't realize it yet. In this world you are neutral among the chaos and the serene. Your travels have taught you more than any biblical text or corporate deviant."

The Fool, although her words were cryptic, knew exactly what she meant. He felt a surge of hope disperse throughout his body, experiencing the bursting of synapses as neurons communicated in furious banter. It was as though the Holy Spirit touched his soul and redemption reigned free. He was ready for the journey the clairvoyant promised, regardless of the prize at the end.

"Where do I start this journey and how will I know where to go?" he asked with excitement in his voice.

"Head onward toward the street, in a North West direction. From there, you will encounter the major arcana, the magician, the high priestess, the empress and emperor, the hierophant, the lovers, the chariot, justice, the hermit, the wheel of fortune, strength, the hanged man, death, temperance, the devil, the tower the start, the moon, the sun, judgment, and the world," she said in one long breath. They will be your map. They will be your guides. If you traverse the path unmolested by their intervention, you shall achieve the small victory that I offer you."

The fool was not sure what the woman's words meant, but was intrigued by the idea of adventure. He thanked her for the card and tucked it neatly into his breast pocket before shaking her hand and wishing her a good evening. In return, she simply smiled and nodded her head before disappearing into the doorway as it closed behind her.

He threw back the last few gulps of his coffee and took the paper cup to the dumpster to dispose of before heading North West toward his journey. He wondered what awaited him, a little extra bounce in his limping step, and paid little attention to the morose surroundings as he shoved the paper cup into the warped dumpster lid. As he turned to leave, the sound of dainty footsteps pounded the asphalt behind him. Startled, he turned to see what was there.

A small white dog, a mutt of some sort, mimicked his path and followed his steps. When he stopped, the canine stopped as well, sitting and staring up at him while wagging his tail. The Fool waved the dog off and continued onward, still hearing the steps but paying little attention as he expected the dog to go his own way when it became bored.

The muffled alley sounds exploded as he stepped out onto the city sidewalk. Beeping horns bellowed amongst the drunken banter outside the late night eateries, mixed with the backdrop of police sirens and call girls selling their flesh laden wares. The Fool stood tall and inhaled the toxic pollution that filled the air.

Not sure which direction to travel from there, he observed the activity on the street. To his right, there the nightlife was rather tame. Only a few men stood about smoking cigarettes and debating the existence of the perfect woman. On his left, a bounty of people lined the sidewalk with a plethora of personalities and personal agendas. Nearly half way down the block, a man in a Santa hat stood at a rickety card table, surrounded by gasping onlookers. The Fool decided to take a gander at the scene.

As he neared, the man was holding a deck of playing cards in his hand, requesting a pretty girl to choose one and show it to the crowd. She placed it back in the deck and in turn he tossed them into an old top hat. He reached his hand deep inside, pulling out a white rabbit. Clenched tightly between the rabbit's teeth was the woman's card. The crowd gasped and cheered, throwing crinkled dollar bills and loose change into the hat.

The Fool, chuckling under his breath said, *"That must be my magician."*

Rather than wait for the next trick, The Fool continued onward, glancing back to see the white dog still right upon his heels. He shook his head in disbelief, continuing onward to find his high priestess.

He was largely unnoticed by the plethora of prostitutes, drug dealers, drunks, and miscreants that lined the street. He had nothing they desired, his true worth concealed by a cloak of invisibility in their eyes.

Near the end of the block, as he prepared to cross the street, a gang of hoodlums clouded the corner as they toked on their marijuana cigarettes. The cloud hung in the air in all its toxicity, pushing them higher into their faded pinnacle of life. It was none of his business, although he loathed the thought of recreational highs, so he attempted to ignore them and their partaking of the Christmas greens.

As he stood, waiting for the street light to change, a woman coughed nearby. The Fool waved away some of the smoke and noticed an aged nun sitting on a nearby bench, cloaked in her midnight blue habit with her hands folded neatly upon her lap. Beside her was a stack of religious pamphlets, piled neatly and ready to give to anyone that needed Jesus.

"Excuse me, Sister," he said. "Would it be too much if I helped you across the street so you can escape the smoke fumes?"

"That would be a splendid idea," she responded.

The Fool took her by the arm and stood at the corner until the light turned green. A large green sedan blasted its horn because they were not walking fast enough. Both The Fool and the nun ignored the sound and continued to the bench on the opposite corner. He helped her sit, worried she might stumble upon her shaky legs and began to walk away.

"Kind sir," she said. "Are you a son of Christ?"

"I was once," he said with his head hung in shame.

"But you are not anymore?" she asked, her vibrant blue eyes piercing his soul.

"I guess I still am, I've just not thought about it in a long while," he hoped his words would halt her prying.

"I see," she said while grabbing a pamphlet. "I've not given any of these out tonight, would you please take one? You don't have to read it, I will just feel better knowing I offered and you accepted."

The Fool took the pamphlet and folded it in half, placing it in his breast pocket next to the fool tarot card. He felt weird, as though he was committing a mortal sin, but did so anyway, giving the nun a smile and a nod of the head before walking onward toward his next destination. The nun traced a cross upon her chest and waved him goodbye.

The Fool felt satisfied and fulfilled for doing the good deed and walked a bit taller toward his next destination. He was wandering aimlessly toward an unknown destination at nearly 1:00 in the morning; still he felt he his mission had a greater purpose of some sort.

As he walked, the bumping sound of bass echoed from the gay club down the way. The Fool always envied the people inside, they were always cheerful and full of confidence. He often wondered if he would be accepted inside if he sipped on a glass of water and watched them dance, but he dared not go in uninvited for fear of being thrown out onto the pavement.

As he approached the club, the paper covered windows did not allow a voyeur to peek inside. However, the door burst open, spilling out a male and female impersonator. The male, dressed as a woman, screamed out, "I'm the only queen you'll ever need to know." To which the female, dressed as a male, replied, "Then I guess that makes me your king?"

They were obviously intoxicated, as evident by their boisterous banter and staggering steps, but The Fool decided to approach them and ask a question.

"Are you the emperor and empress?" he was careful to be respectful.

"Honey, we'll be anything you want us to be, except for straight," said the female impersonator.

Both started to laugh hysterically and high five one another as the door opened behind them. The boisterous queen changed the topic and shoved The Fool out of the way.

"Make way for the pope, dear street man," she was laughing louder than before. "The Hierpohant has made his presence known."

A man, or was it a woman, dressed in a long robe and pointy pontiff's hat exited the bar waving his hands and blessing passersby with Christmas amens. He handed The Fool a fake ten-dollar bill with Jesus' face on the front and scripture on the back. The Fool couldn't help but chuckle as he tucked the bill into his breast pocket along with the other trinkets. Whether coincidence or fate, the characters he met were entertaining at most.

He didn't stick around long; the boisterous behavior was too much for him to take in all at once. Instead, he continued onward to the next corner, where a young couple sat on a bench holding hands and staring longingly into each other's eyes. He wanted to approach them and ask if they were lovers, but the arrival of a horse drawn carriage ushered them from their seats and into the awaiting chariot.

He could feel his heart beat fast as he basked in the presence of young love. He remembered being in love once, a longtime prior, and hoped their life would end much better than his did. As they were ushered away by the carriage, he glanced over to their seat and noticed the white dog sitting in their spot, pawing at a piece of paper on the bench.

He approached the dog, patting it on the head, and took the colorful piece of paper into his hand. On the front was a crude drawing of a heart with the words *I love you* writing inside. On the back, the question *will you marry me* was printed with two boxes with the words *yes* and *no* behind them. The yes box had a check mark inside.

The Fool put the card in his pocket, along with his other trinkets of the night and walked away with a tear in his eye. "Onward to justice," he shouted into the air with an increased gait in his step.

He walked for a couple of blocks without seeing another soul, wondering whether he took a wrong turn or if the night was nothing more than coincidence. *"I guess the mind believes what it wants,"* he said to himself inside his head as he came upon a dark alley.

During his time on the streets, he learned never to head on into an alleyway without peering inside and checking out the surroundings first. Too often he witnessed the aftermath of the creeps that lingered within and the tragedy that corrupted the sanctity of the hidden refuges. Standing with his ear twisted around the corner of the building, his eyes peering into the darkness, he noticed an elderly gentleman slumped over in a pool of water runoff from the nearby downspout, muttering something indecipherable to himself.

The Fool, sensing the alley was safe to enter, walked with gentile strides toward the old man, approaching with caution. As he neared, he could see the man was picking bugs from the cobbled ground and popping them into his mouth, chewing the best he could with his toothless gums. He cringed with each bitter bite, while searching for the next delicacy to sample.

"Sir, are you the hermit?" asked The Fool.

"Wha…heh…me?" he said with a whistle in his voice. "I s'pose I've been called worse."

The man barely batted an eye as he searched out another morsel to soothe his growling belly. He found a rather large daddy long leg, grasped it between his thumb and forefinger and shoved it in his mouth. The spider resisted, extending its legs across the man's lips in protest of its own death, but defeat was inevitable.

"Sir, why are you out here, why not head to the soup kitchen for a meal?" asked The Fool.

"Don't wanna," he snapped. "Don't need their poisons and hate. I take care of me, live off the land, make my own way. That building's boiler is just under this alley, keeping these tasty morsels active all winter long. God gives me this meal and I ain't never denied God."

The message sounded just like the one in The Fool's head, one he preached internally every day. He felt a lump grow in his chest and throat, wondering if the hermit was his destiny. He stood staring at the old man as he shivered in the night, wondering what he could do to make him a little more comfortable. He had a couple cans of beans in his duffle, but worried the man would not take it as anything less than an insult.

While he contemplated how to assist the hermit, resulting in the fairest decision for the scenario, the hermit did not seem to notice he was still there. The night's fresh dusting of snow filled the chilling air, sending spasmic shivers over the old man's body. The Fool felt bad for the man, concerned he would stay the night in the same spot, ignoring the cold. He dropped his duffel onto the cobblestone and grunted to his knees. He rifled through the bag and pulled out a fleece throw blanket, warm and soft against the flesh. He didn't say a word as he stood up again and draped the small blanket over the hermit's back and walked away toward the street.

"You asked if I was a hermit," the man's voice shattered the silence. "I'd ask if you are justice, sentencing me to warmth and comfort, if only fer a night."

The Fool felt a smile drape across his lips as he continued onward without a look back, his body feeling energized by the adrenaline of his good deed. He used the newfound burst to quicken his pace and search out the wheel of fortune, expecting to see an old game show on a shop television set. Instead, he found another flyer, taped to a shop window, offering counsel for people stuck in a never-ending cycle of poor choices, promising to guide their souls toward positive decisions and actions. As with the others, he pulled it from the window and folded it neatly before placing it into his breast pocket with the other pamphlets.

"Rather easy find," he said to himself.

As he stared into the window, The Fool saw his reflection. His face was weary and wrinkled, masking youth with premature aging. His skin was dirty, his hair greasy, clothing filthy and tattered. Yet, within his eyes, the very same that stared back at him, he witnessed the strength of a man that wanted to make the world a better place, to demand the defeat of hatred and bigotry, where all age, sex, religion, and race could live in unity and cohesion; the man with the strength to fight the biggest lie, to defy war that forgot world peace.

He didn't know how long he stared; time meant nothing to him as he wandered the streets. It wasn't until a peculiar motion swayed in the reflection that his gaze wandered and his head twisted behind him. In an instant, his serene contemplation turned to fear and fright as he witnessed a young man, dressed in slacks and a button up shirt, hanging from the nearest light pole by his necktie.

The thrashing body begged for savior, although his mouth could not utter the words. Without thinking, The Fool rushed over to his aid. Yet, his arrival was too delayed as the twitching youngster's breath left his body, releasing his soul into the night. Still, he struggled to release the boy from his hanging death, searching the night for someone to call the police so his family could be found. The street was empty, except for one soul standing in the shadow of the alleyway behind the boy's streetlight.

His presence was only revealed with each drag on a cigarette, the red glow accentuating his devilish features. The fool called out to him, begging for him to phone the police. In response an eerie laugh echoed upon the empty streets. The Fool was able to release the boy from his gallows and rest him upon the ground, within a soft flower bed. A business card fell from the boy's pocket. Without thought, The Fool grabbed the card and noticed the boy's image, along with the address and phone number of his workplace; his title was salesman. The back of the card had an image of the temperance tarot, symbolizing balance, patience, and purpose, all qualities a good salesman desired.

He shoved it in his own breast pocket, and ran for his own life, fearing the devil would extract vengeance upon his soul.

The Fool ran as fast as he could, toward the Foudre Tower, the largest building in town. He knew, regardless of the time of night, someone would be there to call the police, perhaps an officer himself would answer his own call to bring someone to give the boy the respect he deserved.

He ran until he could run no more, his lungs burning with painful conflagrations. His heart pounded with concerning intensity as he leaned against the window of a darkened café. Looking toward the direction he arrived from, he saw he was alone, the devil did not follow. Still, fright consumed his vessel. He wanted to continue to run away from his fears and his insecurities, pushing bravery and strength aside, choosing flight over fight. But, alas, he had no more ability to flee left within. He wanted to collapse to the ground, to become the worriless hermit, to hide within his own head, and become buried under the falling snow.

Just as he was about to give in to his thoughts, the building across the street lit up from within. Painted upon the three large windows were a star, the moon, and the sun. He cocked his head to the side and wiped his eyes with the palms of his hands. Curiosity took over and he walked forward to the front door, crossing the street without looking for oncoming traffic or fear of impeding harm.

He reached for the door handle, but stopped short as he read three simple words on the door, *"No Judgment Zone"*. Without further hesitation, he pulled the door outward and walked inside. There was a collection of mismatched chairs scattered within the lobby, and a woman appeared behind a patchwork counter, summoned by the sound of the three bells above the threshold.

"Welcome, what brings you in?" her sweet voice was like that of an angel.

"I'm not sure, I guess it was my fateful journey," he said without realizing what he was saying.

"Before I can go further, please empty your pockets into this bucket. We need to make sure there are no weapons or drugs," she said almost embarrassed and afraid of accusation.

"No worries," he said in return. "All I have are these pamphlets and flyers."

The woman rummaged through the papers, intrigued by the eclectic collection. She picked up the fool's card last, holding it up in front of her face, examining both sides with great focus.

"The fortune teller told me you would show up," she said. "She saw something in you and begged me to come in early and wait for your arrival.

"That fortune teller, you know her?" he asked.

"Only from a reading I had two nights ago," she said. "The woman begged me, nearly in tears, to open early today and await your arrival. She described you in great detail. I thought she was nuts, but couldn't sleep last night and had to come in, if only to ease my curiosity."

"Why me?" he asked.

"Not sure," she replied. "But, you seem to have an interest in faiths and people of all sorts.

Have you any interest in sharing your journey and helping others find their path?"

The Fool stood speechless, a tear in his eyes.

"It doesn't pay much, but there is a small apartment upstairs, one bedroom, a kitchen, bath, and small living room."

"It sounds like a dream," his voice trailed off.

"I don't know why, but I feel like the position has been empty, waiting for you. I might regret it, but I need you here. The clients need you here."

The woman took The Fool's bag from his shoulder and guided him to the back room where a fresh pot of coffee just finished brewing. The smell wafted through the air, smelling of morning hope. She poured a cup for The Fool and carried his bag to a doorway that led upstairs and hung it upon a hook. A name was stitched into the fabric, the same monotone green as the bag.

"Your name's Joseph?" she asked.

"Not for a long time," he said. "But it sure does feel good to hear it again."

"Nice to meet you, I am Mary."

Twelve Nights

On the first night of Christmas my true love gave to me, partridge in a pear tree. Unknowingly, she also gave me an unexpected gift which was hidden within the leafy branches. It wasn't until nighttime that it reared its ugly head.

I reached for an unripe pear to snack on before sleep. That is when the rabid squirrel woke from its disease ridden slumber. Foaming at the mouth, it hungered for my taste. The scent of my flesh awakened his mind, as he bit down hard on my digit. Blood flowed free, as the poison sunk in, producing fever, headache, and anxiety. I ran from his violence, but his little legs were fast, as he climbed my leg and up my torso, finally tangling within my bushy hair.

I fought to pull him from within my locks, my struggles entangling him deeper and tighter. He squirmed and jerked, strangling himself in the unconventional noose of hair, his foaming spittle moistening the knots, and drying to sticky glue. To release the beast, I scrambled to find alternate means.

Towards the kitchen I stumbled as confusion set in. I grabbed for the shears that we used to cut meat, lopped off my hair, and the squirrel fell to my feet. It seemed to fall for eternity, as the room distorted and contracted. Hallucinations began as I noticed my cats begging at their food dishes.

They morphed into squirrels that taunted me with their hungry meows; I was not in the mood so I hunted them down, scissors still in hand. I latched onto poor Fifi, she didn't know what was coming, and stabbed her through the eye. Looking for the other, I turned to the door where my wife met me with a frown.

She pushed me to the floor, where I hit my head. I blacked out quickly, as her screams faded within my darkness. An un-restful slumber welcomed me, damning me in my dreams. I did wake up, wife sobbing beside me, holding the twitching dead tree rodent. My hair still tangled around its neck, she realized her mistake.

She promises to make it up in the morning, with a new gift to present. But not before a visit the hospital to receive a series of shots. I hoped tomorrow would be better, but found the night would only get worse.

As antibiotics and pain killers flowed through my veins, the nagging twitch of discomfort penetrated to my very soul. The government approved poisons only concealed the damnation gushed within my veins. Traditional twelve days of gifts ended with only one as the battle against rabies was fought within sterile grounds. Each day she visited, her eyes swollen with regret and sorrow. Each day I faded, my mind lost in decay. Oh how I hoped for a Christmas miracle as seizures shook me toward eternal sleep. My only miracles were her visits and knowing she still loves me.

As I reached my final breaths, here I am alone in a darkened room, the lights of beeping machines the only reminder that I am still alive. I twist my head toward the open window, where the snow falls gently upon the world outside. I feel finality creep upon me. Sadness devours me as I realize she won't be here for my final breath. Yet, I know she loves me and that is all I need as the church bells bellow outside signaling Christmas Day has finally arrived.

It's been twelve nights and I can finally close my eyes.

Last Christmas

Through the crumbled fortitude of society, radio silence reminds that the end is near. Although I've kept tick marks upon the wall, the passing days mean nothing more than a aide-mémoire that time still passes despite the world's end. Yet, the farce of normalcy remains as I hold fast to traditions of old for the benefit of my wife and kids.

As the concept of time continues on, radiation poison continues to seep into our existence. One by one, we fell under its weight. As we our way of life became less significant within the dying world, the farce of living becomes harder to maintain. As I look upon the wall, where time is scribbled in marker and crayon, I trace my fingers upon the gravestones scrawled over the horrendous dates. Wife and children faded within time, the final remaining reason to continue lying in bed with a blood-tainted cough. The fever continues to fry the mind; living is only real through the breaths within.

December 25th, I cannot remember the year, has arisen once again and I've a final gift to give. Through the pain and suffering that the cruelty of fate has gifted us, I cry tears of sorrow as my child's pain becomes my own. I kneel before the side of the bed, grasping the grey-skinned hand within my own. My other palm rests upon the sweat-soaked hair as the rasped inhalations struggle to maintain hold on the soul. I pray, although religion escapes me, that peace will once again behold the fragile soul as I reach down to the cloth bundle at my feet. Still holding my child's hand, I unravel the package with other and remove the syringe from within.

An old friend of mine, once a doctor, shared the mortal cocktail before he died, promising me its contents would bring finality and peace when needed. I've used it before, as my loved ones faded; a final dosage contained within.

A kiss upon the forehead seared my chapped lips as I pressed the needle within the only vein I can find. I prop my child into my arms and hold tightly as tears erupt into sobs and the snarled breaths fade to silence. I scream to the air, demanding answers from the invisible God as to why he has chosen to hate his beloved creations.

Why innocence was not saved? Why compassion ceased to remain?

As the fever fades to cold and pink lips rot to purple, I kiss my child's forehead again. The last present given on this last Christmas was one of freedom from pain and agony. The final rest is my final gift as I carry my child outside where the fresh dug grave awaits eternal slumber. It is cold and the ground is freezing, but I choose to sleep where my wife and kids rest, spending one last night at their side before the calendar starts anew, with no celebratory landmarks to remind of life before this last Christmas as I continue to exist alone.

Why did the Chicken Cross the Road?

Old man winter's frigid tears fell upon the public park's landscape, hiding the green grasses beneath. The sun's gaze upon the frozen pond diminished as he retreated under the horizon to sleep, leaving December's cold moon to take his spot within the starry sky. The dimming light cast shadows of the naked trees across the virginal snow; their limbs stretched into contorted and unnatural shapes as they meandered over windblown drifts of snow.

Upon the frozen pond, the moon's glow was accentuated by illuminated lamps, casting light upon the plethora of ice skaters that glided across the shimmering rink. The air filled with laughter and casual chatter, with the occasional whimpering from a child that fell upon his or her behind, and the wafting smell of hot cocoa and coffee. Winter had arrived in the small town of Mishawaka and families from all around gathered to celebrate its embrace.

Looking down upon the celebratory shindig, a lanky man dressed only in a flannel shirt and jeans, sat hunched upon a nearby hill with his elbows propped upon his lap, his head resting upon his shivering palms. His presence was unnoticed by everyone below, his body hidden in the shadows of the oncoming night. The hours spent in the seat were evident by the blanket of snow that hid all but the top of his well-worn sneakers. Despite the cold air that tickled the skin within his loose flannel and gray t-shirt inside, he did not seek warmth or companionship from the town's people below.

Darkened bags collected underneath his bloodshot eyes; tear tracks stained his cheeks. His mind, a whirlwind of chaotic thought, lacked focus and the ability to concentrate long enough to make sense of his condition. So, he sat nearly motionless, but for the shivering, waiting for his fate to take hold.

The world around him was dark, detail invisible to his cognition. Although focused on the families below, he did not see them, hear them, or smell the flagrant air that approached his nostrils. He was lost in his own world, as dark as it had become. His condition left him unaware of the stranger that arrived at his side, sitting next to him on the cold metal park bench.

The stranger, a jolly old man with hair as white as an angel's soul, removed his heavy coat and draped it over the man's back, blocking his pale flesh from winter's onslaught. He pulled it tight enough to garner a response as warmth reentered the man's body.

"Young man," said the stranger. "Are you alright?"

The man turned his head and glared at the stranger, not saying a word.

"The strong silent type, I see," said the stranger with a chuckle.

For a time, neither wore a watch so they didn't know how long, they sat side by side in silence. The young man focused on the nothingness he created in front of him, the stranger enjoying the exuberant occasion down upon the frozen pond. From time to time he would glance at the young man, his smile concealing concern behind his eyes, until the young man took notice.

"Seriously, old man," he grunted. "Can you just leave me the fuck alone? I'm trying to think."

The stranger did not seem fazed by the foul language. "My apologies, I just saw you here shivering without proper garments for this cold night, and thought I would lend you my coat and maybe an ear."

"Well, it isn't necessary," said the young man as he finally looked up and really saw the man for the first time. "Great. Of all people, I get Santa Clause to barge into my business. What's the matter, everyone down there having so much fun, none of them sitting in your lap?"

"Please," said the old man in a forgiving tone. "Call me Chris. I was just on my way past you and thought I'd check to see if you were okay, you looked to be in need of a friend."

"Chris," he said with a sarcastic chuckle. "Yeah, of course. Who the fuck else would you be? And friend? Hah, what sort of shit is that. Ain't no one my friend in this town. Not even my own fucking wife"

Chris, seeing the young man still shivering, unraveled his scarf from around his neck. He began to reach out and drape it over his newfound companion's cold body, but decided to offer it to him instead.

"Can I ask your name?" inquired Chris as he placed the scarf into the man's hands.

"It's a free fucking world," he responded, staring at the red velour garment. "Just call me John. John Doe."

"Well John," said Chris. "Seems you have a story to tell, and I have a fantastic ear for such things."

John looked up from the scarf and glared in Chris' direction. "You wanna hear my fucking story? Well pull up a fucking chair, because I have a story to tell."

Chris shifted in his seat, turning his body toward John, his head cocked to the side. "Sometimes, telling the story relieves the tension inside and makes everything better."

"Well, it is too late for better," John's tone was angry as his voice rattled under the cold. "What the fuck, though. Hell, you'll probably be the last to hear it anyway; might as well tell my story to Santa Claus, as if this day isn't screwed up enough."

Chris was not a fan of John's swearing, as was evident by the scowl upon his face. He tried to hide it, but his smile was an obvious farce. "Please, tell me everything. If I can, I'll do everything in my power to make it all better."

"As long as that shit doesn't mean I am going to become a fucking elf, I'm game for anything. But, I guarantee you can't save me like some Jesus shit."

Chris did not respond. Instead, he crossed his hands upon his lap and waited for John to start. He watched as John's shivers continued, despite the heavy velvet coat and scarf; his breathing was heavy and a tear would sneak out of his eyes every so often. He held back the urge to offer a tissue, not wanting to overstep his boundaries and push John away.

"Hell, I'll never see you again, so why the fuck not," said John, pulling the coat tight to his frame. "Ask anyone in this fucking town, I'm a legend. Not for being the good guy, but for being the party guy. Everyone thinks I'm an asshole, good for nothing, just a piece of shit that is good to be the life of the party. So, that is what I am to them. No one cares what I want; they'd just laugh at me and tell me that my dreams are not achievable, maybe buy me another beer and wait for the next crazy and drunken stunt I'd pull."

Chris interrupted. "What is your dream, John?"

"Who the fuck cares what I dream of?" retorted John.

"I do," said Chris.

"Well, shit. I want to be the best goddamn dad to my kids, provide for them, but most of all, always be there for them. My kids mean everything to me, but every time I turn around, something takes me away from them."

"Like what?" asked Chris.

"Hell, I've traveled to other states looking for work, been to jail a few times, but most of all, the fucking bar keeps calling my name and taking me away from them. I ain't ever cheated on my wife, but the bar, well, she is my mistress."

"So," said Chris. "You are an alcoholic?"

"Only when I am there," said John. "Any other time, I don't even want a drink. But, the bar is where I can let off steam, to get away. Funny thing is, I don't spend a dime when I am there. Everyone buys me my drinks, just to see what shit

I'll get into. Hence, being a legend in this fucking town."

"Then why go to the bar at all," asked Chris. "It seems like staying home with your wife and kids is the best place for you."

"Yeah?" asked John. "Well, tell that to my fucking wife. Sometimes I think she starts shit on purpose, just to get me out of the fucking house. I can't stay there when she shows her shit. I'd fucking explode. I ain't never hit a woman, but she pushes me to the edge sometimes. So, I go to the fucking bar."

"I see," said Chris.

"Do you, fucking do you?" The veins in John's forehead were showing as he shouted at Chris.

"Everyone has a catalyst for anger," said Chris in a somber tone. "I can see that you are a giving soul. You'd give the shirt off of your back for anyone in need, just as I have done for you. Yet, people take advantage of you, use it to their advantage, for their entertainment. It is not fair to you, yet you allow it to continue because you are afraid of being alone. Still, you are always alone, at least in your head. It seems to me, the only brightness in your days is your children."

"Fucking right they are," said John, a tear falling from his eye. "I'm so scared they are going to grow up like me. So, I run from them, hide at the bar. The less they see me, the less likely they'll pick up my bad habits. Right?"

"Isn't being away from them just as bad?" asked Chris. "Why not forget about everyone else and just live for your kids?"

"Ha," chuckled John. "Too late for that shit now."

"How so?" asked Chris, leaning in closer to John.

"My fucking wife, the woman that is supposed to love me through thick and thin, fucking gave me divorce papers today. From the looks of it, she gets full custody and I get to see my beautiful kids once a fucking month," the tears started flowing. "I know that isn't final, but what judge will side with a fuck off like me, especially in this fucking hell hole."

"What about looking on the bright side?"

John clenched his teeth as he jumped from his seat, dropping the coat and scarf to the ground. His legs were like jelly and he fell to the ground, sobbing.

Chris reached down and tried to help John back to his seat, but he resisted. His skin was reddening and he was breaking out in a cold sweat.

To the touch, he was burning up. Chris simply lifted the coat from the snow and draped it over John where he lay, hoping the snow would give relief to his internal heat.

"You know what happened after she gave me the papers?" he was still sobbing, wiping his eyes with the sleeve of his flannel. "I fucking blew up, right in front of my kids. I punched a hole in the wall, only missing her face by an inch. My fucking kids saw it happen! They have never seen me like that. It fucking destroyed me!"

Chris wanted to reach down and give John a hug, but held back, giving him a chance to let it all out. "Go on, tell me more. What did you do next?"

John lay back, as though he were about to make a snow angel. "I did what I always do when she starts shit. I ran to the door."

John's tears erupted as he started to cry uncontrollably. He contorted into the fetal position, his back toward Chris. His body shook uncontrollably; to the point that Chris thought he might be having a seizure. Then, John spoke again. "Then, you know what happened?"

"Please, tell me," said Chris.

"As I was grabbing my coat and gloves, my son ran to me. He told me not to cry, telling me that everything would be okay. You know how hard that was? I couldn't look him in the eye, I just grabbed the door knob as I unclasped the lock. Just before I opened it, he said he would tell me a joke."

"What joke did he tell you?" asked Chris.

"He asked, 'why did the chicken cross the road?'"

"A classic," replied Chris.

"I asked him why."

"Did he give you a funny answer?" asked Chris.

"No, with tears in his eyes, he said, 'To get to the other side'," said John, erupting into tears again.

"That isn't so bad," said Chris. "He knew you were upset, that you needed a laugh to lighten you up."

John sat up again, looking at Chris with bloodshot and tear filled eyes. "I left out a key part of that story."

"I felt that you might have. Care to tell it now?" asked Chris.

"After nearly punching my wife in the face, I ran to the bathroom and stared at myself in the mirror. On the other side of the door, she screamed at me, calling me everything from a loser to a fuck up. She told me that every time I ran to the bar with my tail between my legs, she called my friend Tony over to fuck him; to know what it was like to feel a man between her legs. I wanted to open the door and break her fucking neck and shit down her throat. But, I couldn't do that to my kids. She loves them, and they need her. So, I did the only thing I could. I grabbed three bottles of prescription pills and chewed them all down, some I swallowed whole. Then I threw open the door and ran to grab my coat."

"Oh my," said Chris as he sat down in the fluffy snow next to John.

"Yeah," he said, his body going limp as he braced himself against Chris' body. "All I ever wanted was to be there for my kids, always at their side when they were scared or in trouble and here I go and fucking kill myself."

"You said you had your coat and gloves," said Chris, holding John close to his side, trying to keep him warm as the overdose took its hold.

John's speech became choppy and shaky. "I gave them to a homeless man on my way here. He needed them more than I do."

"As I said earlier," Chris new the end was near. "You are the type to give the shirt off your back to those in need."

"Yet," John took a deep breath. "I can't help myself. I guess, just like the chicken, I'm about to get to the other side."

A tear spilled from Chris' eye as John exhaled for the last time. He sat there, holding the stranger in his arms, knowing that somehow, some way, he needed to help John's kids through the hard time, especially at Christmas. Not completely sure how he could help. He held John's cold body close, raised a finger to his nose, and looked toward the sky.

Where the pair sat, an indentation in the snow was all that remained.

***

Christmas morning arrived in Ellington upon the flutter of a few snowflakes and a gentle breeze. Few mourned the disappearance of John, the legend. Everyone assumed he simply left town and would stroll back into the city limits when he felt everything had blown over. No one knew of his tragic fate upon the hill that overlooked ice covered pond.

At the home of John's children, his son looked out the living room window, hoping to spot his father's footprints outside, only to be disappointed at a pristine layer of snow upon the sidewalk. His daughter, still too young to understand what had happened that night, danced anxiously in front of the Christmas tree. Her excitement drew his son away from the window and to her side. In his little mind, he promised himself that he would be there to protect his sister, and that he would always be the man he knew his father was.

At his mother's beckon, he handed his sister a box wrapped in pink, grabbing a bright red wrapped box for himself. His sister shouted as she pulled out the baby doll she wanted from the commercial; he took his time unwrapping the gift that was wrapped like no other. Inside, tissue paper was neatly folded around two small figures. The first was a small action figure, about six inches tall, wearing a jacket similar to his father's. The figure's hair was eerily familiar and its watchful eyes seemed to stare deep into his soul. The next figure was a small rubber chicken, flattened as most practical joke props were.

John held the two figures close to his chest as tears fell from his eyes. His mother, trying to keep the mood positive asked him what was wrong, why was he crying.

"He knew he couldn't be here, so he did what he had to do, to make sure he would be here," he said.

"What is that?" asked his mother, no idea what her sweet boy was talking about.

"To get to the other side mommy," he said with a smile upon his face. "To get to the other side."

About Essel Pratt

Essel Pratt is a purveyor of horror and fantasy, conjuring tales that haunt souls and inspire imagination. As a student of psychology and teller of tales, Essel writes to share the complex nature of his imaginings with the world. His ever-expanding catalog of short stories spans multiple anthologies and collections, ranging from whimsical fantasy to bizarre horror, including everything in between. Dedicated fans have praised his creations, labeling his talents as prolific in substance

Hailing from Mishawaka, Indiana, his passion for writing began in the early years as his imagination taunted from within, begging for a release.

Dabbling in art at first, he found that the stories that pleaded to be told could not be imprisoned by ink and paint alone. His most notable and prevalent accomplishments include Final Reverie, Sharkantula, and the multiple short stories that have garnered a following of their own, such as the adventures of Detective Mansfield.

Inspired by C.S. Lewis, Clive Barker, Stephen King, Harper Lee, William Golding, and many more, Essel doesn't restrain his writings to straight horror, instead exploring the blurred boundaries of horror within its competing genres, mixing the elements into a literary stew.

Also Available from Essel Pratt

- ❖ Final Reverie
- ❖ Sharkantula
- ❖ Slothantula
- ❖ Trailer Park Quarantine
- ❖ Curse of the Killer Toilet Paper
- ❖ 13 Middle Grade Tales of Fantasy and Terror
- ❖ Reaper: Act One
- ❖ Attack of the B-Movie Horrors
- ❖ Xperimental Genocide
- ❖ Lacrimation of the Leviathan
- ❖ Backwoods Bonfire
- ❖ Yeti, Yearning
- ❖ Ungodly Undoing
- ❖ Repercussions Run Rampant
- ❖ Orleans Occult
- ❖ Poetic Despair
- ❖ Secession Part One: Voluntary Deportation
- ❖ Secession Part Two: Victims of the Wall Poetic Despair
- ❖ Harambe and the Very Bad Day
- ❖ ABCs of Zombie Friendship

❖ Guide to Being a Successful Facebook Admin

You can follow Essel at the following:

www.facebook.com/esselprattwriting

Esselpratt.blogspot.com

@EsselPratt

http://esselpratt.wixsite.com/darknessbreaks

If you like what you read in this book, please consider leaving a review

45610041R00129